1.

May 2018

The wet suit protected her body from the water, but her scalp pricked with the cold saltiness of it. She drifted on her back, looking up at the wide blue sky. She floated, letting her mind open and flow with the gentle undulation of the waves. Until a big golden retriever splashed past her with a ball in its mouth, and, she could have sworn, a smile.

Turning onto her front, she swam towards the beach, standing up before she got there, and wading through the surf and onto the warm sand. Her hair hung wet around her face and she pushed it back, liking the dribbling sensation, already drying as the stiff breeze hit her face.

"Julia, come and have a coffee." She turned towards the voice, and saw Amanda waving wildly. She smiled back, and walked to the small café.

"I was going to phone you today, I'm glad you're here. I got an offer." She peeled herself out of the top half of her wet suit, the empty arms dangling near her knees.

"Really? A good one?" Amanda gestured to the counter to bring another coffee.

"Yes. Full asking price, plus an extra ten thousand if I can be out by the end of May. They want the summer takings." Julia sat down on the empty chair at the table. Her coffee arrived and she sipped, it was lovely.

"That's three weeks. Too fast, tell them you need longer." Amanda planted her elbows on the table, her bottom lip sticking out.

"I don't though. I really don't Am." She reached across the table. "I'm going home to pack, and then they can have it." It was true, she had only to worry about herself. That gave her freedom, but also some lonely moments. "I'm ready to go."

"Where are you going to live though?"

"I don't know yet, so once I've accepted the offer, I am going to have a look. I can always put my stuff into storage while I find somewhere." Julia shrugged. She felt her good mood slipping away as the details and downsides of the deal were pointed out.

"It'll be somewhere near here though? You love being able to swim every day in the sea, and walking on the beach." Amanda sipped her coffee. Julia watched her sip. They weren't best friends, but Amanda had been so supportive when Julia's relationship had fallen apart, Amanda's marriage had been going through a rough patch at the same time, so they had helped each other.

"I'll let you know when I find it. Thanks for the coffee, Am." Julia walked back across the sand to her car. She opened the door, peeling her legs out of the rest of her wet suit and throwing it into the back of her car. The lovely drifting feeling was gone, replaced by a niggle of irritation at having to think about her next move. The golden retriever ran past her and dropped the ball at an old man's feet. His tail wagging and his fur dripping onto the sand.

"Good morning. How is the water today?" He sat on the low bench, his shirt and tie slightly incongruous among the swimmers and surfers.

"It's still cold, but wonderful. Your dog enjoyed it. How are you today?" She had no clue what his name was, but he was at the beach most mornings, as she was.

"Are you never worried, the water is deep." His voice was deep and clear, with a hint of an accent.

"I don't go out that far. Are you never tempted, to take a dip?" She rubbed her hair with a towel. He laughed and shook his head. "Have a good day." She climbed into the car, waving and he waved back.

She drove up the hill, to the next turning, and into her home, and holiday lets business. She checked her reflection in the rear-view mirror, not wanting to frighten any guests. Her hair was short and thick, falling in soft waves around her face, and her skin was golden even though it was only May. She threw open the car door and climbed the two steps to her front door. The house was small, she supposed, but she had been happy there. The buyers seemed very keen, and had also stipulated that they wanted all the furniture left. This was fine with her. She hadn't chosen any of it for permanence.

Her phone rang, and she dug in her handbag to find it. It was the estate agent.

"So, with everything going through nicely, where are you thinking about moving to?" He was after all, in the business of selling houses, and she was in need of a home.

"I'm still looking, on the internet, Jonty, but I haven't found anything yet. Don't worry, I won't hold anything up, if I can't find anything in time, I'll have to rent somewhere." Julia folded a pair of trousers, and added them to a pile, her phone lodged between her shoulder and her ear.

"What are you looking for? Something near the beach, or further out?" He flicked through the list of properties on his screen.

"I don't know, I want to be further out, but something different, a bit of a project perhaps? That's the trouble I'm not sure what I'm looking for." She sat down on the window sill, her hands playing with the socks in her hands.

3

"A project? Really?" She could hear the excitement in his voice.

"Why? Do you have something?" She paused with her hand in the drawer.

"Well, it needs a fair amount of work. Do you want to see it?" She wondered if he was holding his breath. "Is today too early? I have a clear afternoon."

"OK, give me the address, and I'll meet you there." She pulled open the bedside cabinet drawer, looking for a pen.

"Don't worry, I'll pick you up. It's a bit off the beaten track, hard to find." He smiled to himself. "Is two o'clock OK?" He hung up, spreading his fingers, and miming jazz hands. She knew he would be. He might be her estate agent, but he was also her friend.

She gave up on the packing and went to find shoes, which she had in a pile in the hallway. Finding two that matched, and made sense for viewing houses was a challenge, but not insurmountable.

A shower, and more packing before she could go and see the new place, seemed in order.

"Jonty? New car?" She opened the passenger door and slid onto the seat. The land rover was old and smelled as though several very large, damp dogs lived in it.

"Not mine, I'm borrowing." He watched the road while he got out of the town. "This property has wonderful views. Not a sea view, but the price is very competitive." He drove onwards. "Right, this is our turning." The road narrowed, and he turned off again. There was grass growing in the middle, and the hedges pushed in from either side.

"This doesn't look like it sees much traffic." She turned towards him.

"It gets better." He laughed, risking a sideways look at her. She settled back in her smelly seat and waited.

They reached a gate, and she hopped out and pushed it open. He drove through and she closed it behind the land rover.

"This is the land. It comes with nearly five acres. Did I mention that?" She nodded. The land rover lurched to the right. "You might want to hold on, it's a bit bumpy."

"This is why the smelly four-wheel drive was necessary?" He nodded. "For god's sake, where are we going? Is this a safari? Will there be lions?"

"Not that I know of. Ah, here we are." The hand brake sounded as though it had not been used for a long time as it clicked and crunched. "Hello Hugo." Jonty shouted. "This is the lady I told you about. This is Julia."

She opened the door and slid down to the ground.

"Hello Julia. Come and have a look." Hugo held his hand out to his side, in a gesture that reminded her of a magician's assistant.

She watched him walk up the hill, his jacket was ripped and his trousers were rolled half way up his calves. She shrugged her shoulders and followed him. The top of the short hill was a revelation. The view was unbroken, except by a small area of woodland. Something that had been tense and knotted up inside her unravelled. She breathed in, and it felt good, it felt amazing.

"What is that?" She pointed to a wall, a little further on.

"It's the house. Or at least one of them. Come and have a look." Jonty joined them at the top of the hill, he was breathing hard.

They walked towards the building.

"Jonty. What the… it has a tree, growing out of roof. No, there's no roof. Jesus Jonty. There's no roof." She turned on her heel. "No roof."

"You'd have to take the tree down, of course." He was nodding, as though he had given her some very wise advice.

"Do you think?" She raised an eyebrow at him.

"Yes. It is a bit short on roofing. Don't judge it on that though. There are three buildings, and there is planning permission to develop them all. That over there will be a five bedroom, this one a two bedroom, and that one over there, that will be a three bedroom." He pointed carefully at the barely standing walls, with no rooves.

Julia stood, studying the whole place. The silence was huge, overwhelmingly enormous. Could she live in that much quiet? Why was she even thinking about it? Was she considering it?

"You have drawings?" She asked Hugo.

"Yes. Do you want to see them?" She nodded, and he marched off. He turned back to her. "Come on then." She followed him, and he disappeared into a shed, coming back out with a roll of papers in his hand. "Here you go."

She sat on the grass and unrolled them, and looked at the drawings. "Do you have copies?" Hugo nodded. "Can I borrow them? Talk to a builder and see how much it will cost?"

"You like it then?" Jonty held her eyes over the drawings.

"I like the views. I like the peace and quiet. The price might be a bit optimistic. I don't know if it's a bit too much of a project for me, and I won't know unless I can get a price for this work, and then think about it. Then maybe get my head examined." She chewed her lower lip, before turning to Hugo. "Are you OK for a builder to come and look?"

"Anytime. Doesn't matter if I'm here or not." Hugo beamed at her. His hair looked as though it had never met a brush, and his clothes were old and shabby. She looked behind him at the shed, where it appeared, he was living.

She nodded and rolled the drawings back up. "Show me the land." Hugo led her away from the buildings, and together they walked around the boundary of the land, the fencing was better in some areas than others, and completely missing in places. There was an area of woodland, and a stream, and more views that made her heart feel different, lighter. Hugo talked most of the time, about the land, the view, his plans to buy a beach bar in Thailand, and his expectation that life with a Thai girlfriend would be huge improvement on any Cornish woman he had ever met.

Jonty was waiting by the land rover when they got back. Hugo waved them off, and they bumped and jolted across the land. Jonty was quiet, waiting for her to talk about it. She couldn't, she had no space left in her head to find words.

"Do you have a builder in mind?" He asked, and noticed how she held the drawings tightly against her body. She nodded, holding the views tight in her head.

"I'll talk to Jamie later, and call you once he's had a look. I know I can trust him, he did the work on my place. I don't suppose it's an easy sell." She bit her lip.

"No, but a developer might be interested. Or someone who wants to make a beautiful home, or a smallholding, or a micro-brewery, I hear those are all the rage." He laughed.

"OK, so I'm a bit transparent. I like the views, Jonty. If I can afford to do the work, I'll make an offer. OK?" She hugged the drawings a little tighter, as he pulled up on her driveway.

"OK. Do you want to come out for dinner with Sam and me?" He smiled across at her. "We could go to the Haymakers, I know you like their food."

"Thanks, lovely, but I want to catch Jamie before he finishes for the day." She opened the door. "This land rover still smells." He laughed out loud and waved as she closed the door.

She scrolled through the numbers on her phone. "Hi Jamie. Any chance you can do a quote for me?"

"Julia? I heard you'd sold your place." She could hear road noise in the background.

"This is something new. It's big. Have you got any time to have a look at the drawings, and the place?" She chewed her lip.

"Um, yes. If you don't mind meeting me early tomorrow morning. About 6.30? Is that too extreme?" His laugh was deep and throaty. "Give me the address and I'll meet you there." She gave him the post code. "Is that Hugo's place?"

"You know him?" Julia was amazed.

"Hugo likes a drink, down at the Bell. I've known him for years. Are you thinking of buying his place? It's a ruin." He paused. "I don't need to see the buildings, I've seen them. Let's meet up and look at the drawings. Are you at home now?" She confirmed that she was. "OK, I'm intrigued. I'll call in. OK?" She agreed and put the kettle on, waiting to pour the coffee when Jamie pulled into the driveway.

He sat with a mug steaming in his hand, and the drawings on the table. "What's the plan?"

"I want to live there. I want to do one building, this one, and turn it into three separate holiday lets, dividing here, and here." She ran her fingers across the drawings. "I'll live in one, and use the income from the other two, to save up to fix up the other two buildings." She watched him carefully. "I might move out of the third through next summer to take the most money I can. Small problem though, I need it watertight before the winter. First thing, before anything else, we need to clear the rocks and make a drive in so we can get building supplies in."

"Can I do some sums and call you tomorrow?" He picked up the drawings and rolled them up. "Julia, are you sure this is what you want?"

"No. I know I want to live there. I understand the holiday let business. I know how to make it a year-round proposition. I need to make it pay its own way." He nodded and waved from the front door.

Her coffee was cooling, so she left it on the table and went out on to the decking. The light that she loved was fading. This bit of the day, this was her best time, to sit and watch the sun disappear. She pulled her cardigan closer as the colours in the sky changed. If she did this, if she moved out onto the moor, would she miss this? Of course, she would, but would she miss it too much to do it? She closed her eyes and pictured the view across the moors, and her lips curved slowly into a smile. The moors felt right, like she had come home. She could visit the beach, if ever she needed to. She watched the rest of the light go, and stayed on the deck, feeling every bit of the fluttering in her stomach, and the breath that caught in her chest.

More than anything she hoped that Jamie's price would be within her budget. Her mobile buzzed. She checked the caller ID, and smiled. "Hey, Lou."

"Hi Julia. How's everything?" There was a little shake in her voice. A waver, that suggested tears.

"You OK?" Julia's eyebrows furrowed a little.

"No. The spa hasn't paid me, for two months, and when I went up there today to chase it up, they said it was a cash flow thing, and they wouldn't be able to pay it, and they won't need me from now on. I've paid my rent, up front, until August, but after that, unless I can get a new job, I'm out of money, and out of a home. I don't know what to do. I know you have fought your way out after troubles, I thought you might be able to tell me what to do." She sniffed, and a sob caught her half way.

"Oh Lou." Julia's heart dipped, she had been so excited, and her friend was in trouble. "Of course, we can find a way out of it. Do you want me to come over? Listen, whatever happens, if you don't have it sorted by the time you need to move, you can stay with me. Wherever I am. OK?"

2.

The town was shabby, his feet itched with needing to be gone. His wife was so happy to be a mother, why he resented her happiness was a mystery to him. He wanted a bigger, better life. He wanted more and richer chances at the better things he dreamed of, the life he knew was within his reach. People moved out of his way as he made his last few purchases and carried them back to the house. They knew him, or knew of him.

"I'm home. I brought some shopping, and a toy for my little soldier." The boy peeped from behind his mother's skirt. There was a lot of skirt, but then, since the child was born, there was a lot of her.

She smiled, that soft, gentle smile, it used to melt his heart; now it just reminded him that she had changed, so much. What was it with women, as soon as a kid arrived, they lost the fire in their soul? He smiled back, but without any warmth. He was thinking about how good it would feel to get away. He crouched down, holding out the toy to his son. The boy reached out to take the little car, his eyes widening as he took its weight into his hands. She stood behind him, nudging a reminder.

"Thank you, Papa." The toy taking his attention.

"I have to go now, or I will miss the train." He ran his hand over the boy's head. "You must look after your Mama. I will be home again soon, and I will bring you a present." His eyes met the boy's and held. There was something there. In a few years, perhaps, once he was older, and not so tied to his mother, things would be different.

"Why do you have to go?" Her voice caught, thick with tears.

"You know why. What I am doing is for all of us. It will buy us a better life. I don't want to leave you both, but I have to, you know that." The easy lie spilled comfortably. "We both have to be strong. Once I'm settled, I will send for you both. A new life sweetheart." He pulled her into his arms, feeling her melt against him. He loved her, he always had. He was irritated by her, but that was just something that happened after years. He kissed the top of her head. "Take care of yourself." He picked up the bag by the door, and he was gone. His head felt clearer, he could breathe better.

The train pulled into the station, and he climbed up the step to board. He watched the country pass the window, and over the next day and night he sat upright and uncomfortable, holding himself awake with his dreams and plans. The ferry he caught from Calais was full of people and he struggled to find somewhere to sit, so he leaned against the rail and watched the waves and the approaching cliffs. Finally, in Dover, he found a cheap place to stay and slept. In the morning he carried his parcel to the meeting and handed it over. He had planned to take his earnings, and leave. He had expected to send some of the money home, and use the rest to set himself up in this new life. But his plans had been changed.

The men who had met him had laughed at him, and told him to leave, without payment. His temper, cold and coiled like a snake, fed by his resentment and by his poverty, smashed his fists through their smirking, fat faces and sliced his blade through their bellies and one throat. His breathing stilled, and he collected his parcel, wiping the blood from it, and the money he should have been paid.

There was a coat hanging outside the door, and he slipped it on, to cover the worst of the blood stains. Outside on the street, the birds sang, and he walked quickly away. He had new plans to make.

He bought new clothes, and caught a train to London. This was the place to start a business. He had a product which people wanted to buy and cash to build a life with. After the pile of bodies were found, his reputation grew amongst the people who knew about the business, and none of that hurt his ability to sell and buy safely. He was one of a new breed of tough criminals. London became his home, and his playground. Women were everywhere, and his mixture of money, danger and drugs, made him a magnet.

He was building a life for himself. The trouble was that there was no room for his wife and child. He had failed in his promise to send for them. His life was a party. He had no time or space for a frumpy wife and a small child. He told himself, when these things bothered him, which was rare, that this was no life for them, they would not be safe.

When he met Janice, she was a surprise. Not just because she was beautiful, they were all beautiful. She was funny, and bright, and she had ideas about the right way and the wrong one. He knew that people who worked for him resented what they saw as her influence. They offered him other women, but he wasn't tempted. He wanted Janice. She was frightened by his life. He told her about the family he had left behind. She couldn't understand how he had left his child. It started him thinking, about the boy, he had been away for nearly a year, and though he sent money home, he had no other contact. They had no address or telephone numbers for him. He sent messages that he was working hard, and told them no details. The child would have grown up a bit, he would be less of a baby perhaps. He had no wish to see his wife, but perhaps there was a way to get custody of his son, bring him up in the new country, in the new ways. Perhaps with Janice.

He knew that his wife would never give up the child. That was something he could be sure of. He plotted, and planned, sharing his thoughts with nobody else. This was something that needed to be undertaken without anybody knowing. He called a man he trusted to him, and told him what was required. Three days later the man returned. He had visited the family home. They had checked locally and it was the right place. The son was not at home, he was, according to neighbours, staying with his aunt. They brought the baby girl though.

He paid them. He always paid his debts. He showed nothing of his feelings to them, but he was angry. This was what he had wanted to avoid, he knew that his wife would not have been unfaithful, she must have been pregnant when he left home. He sat heavily on the sofa and dropped his head into his hands. What was he supposed to do with a baby? A baby who wailed, and screamed all the time. He would have to employ a nanny, if only the child would stop squalling, he would be able to think. There was no option to return the child to her mother. The child stopped, and the relief he felt was huge. He turned to find Janice cradling the baby in her arms. The look on her face struck fear through his body. He had seen that look before. What was it with women, as soon as a baby arrived? Their brains left them entirely.

He watched for a few days as Janice fed and cared for the baby. He watched her face when he talked about getting rid of the child, and saw her eyes become guarded around him. Two weeks later, he knew he had lost her. When she packed up the baby and took her out of his house, in the early hours, he let her go. He watched her walk away, feeling lonelier than he had ever in his life. Not for the baby. At the time he had felt only irritated by the baby, and jealous of the love the child had stolen from him.

He was a powerful man, he kept tabs on Janice, and the child, as she grew. They were happy, he thought, and better off without him. He stopped sending money to his wife. He told people who he knew would tell her, that he was dead, killed for stealing from his boss. He stopped thinking of her or his son. He stopped worrying about her.

He grew older and wiser, and made more money than he needed. He helped his daughter, when he could do so without being noticed. He helped Janice, the only woman he had ever loved as an equal, when she was in difficulty. He spent time finding ways to give her money without her realizing that she was being given anything. It was a challenge. She was smart.

3.

Jamie's price was big, but not more than she had expected. She parked her car at the beach, and watched a single surfer ride a wave in. Was this what she wanted? Making a decision, she started the engine and drove as far as she could without getting a land rover, then climbed out and walked uphill towards the gate, which she could almost see in the distance. The backs of her calves tightened and she pushed her feet harder into the track road, and covered the distance as fast as she could. She felt breathless, not because of the walk, but because of the excitement building inside her. She wanted, no, that was too weak a word, needed, to be back on the land, to see the view. Her view.

Hugo was within shouting distance when she reached the gate, and looked surprised to see her, but waved to her, calling her in. She climbed the gate, and felt her breathing slow.

"Sorry Hugo, I just needed another look." She felt a little lighter as she crossed the space.

"Did you get your prices yet?" Hugo pushed his sleeves up towards is elbows.

"Yes. I have, and they're big. I really want this, but I don't know if it's the best thing or the stupidest thing I've ever done." She ran her fingers through her hair.

"Can't help you on that one." Hugo shook his head. "Why not have a walk round and see if that helps. I have to go out, but, help yourself." He held both his arms out, before he walked to the gate and climbed into the land rover. She turned away, and there was her view, the one she saw when she closed her eyes, and in her dreams. A tear slipped from her eye, and she swiped it with her wrist. The decision was made.

She stood still and felt the peace of the place seeping into her. Her phone beeped. Ah, that answered a question about phone reception. She checked the message, and clicked to dial the number.

"Hey, Jonty. I want to make an offer." She took a breath, and straightened her shoulders. "The building costs will be high so my offer will be a bit lower." She walked back to the gate, discussing the price and finally confirming her offer, providing she could move in when she moved out of her place. She didn't need a surveyor's report, she knew the place was falling down and had no roof.

She rested her hand on the gate. She would be back soon, and it would be hers. The smile that crossed her face was real, and came from somewhere new inside her.

She cooked, expecting Lou for supper, and was pleased when she saw the car pull in. They took time, chatting over the food, and a glass of wine. Lou had managed to get a couple of days a week at a fitness club on the outskirts of town, which was a start, and Julia was bubbling with everything she had planned for her new project. It felt like a bubble filled with excitement, lodged just below her rib cage.

Lou stayed over, falling asleep on the sofa. Julia pulled a throw over her and left her to sleep. She climbed into bed, closed her eyes and the view popped up in front of her again. A smile spread slowly across her face, she fell asleep, feeling as though she was going home.

Hugo agreed to clear out his shed to fit in with her time frame. He also included the Land Rover, which still smelled heavily of wet dog in the sale. She took it to the car wash and scrubbed the whole thing, before lining the back with bin liners and loading her personal possessions in. Her buyers wanted her furniture left, so there wasn't as much as there could be, but it still took three loads.

She scrubbed the shed that would be home until the first building was waterproof. When it smelled like bleach instead of over-ripe socks, she felt better and left it to air. The windows were open, and stayed that way while she went shopping. She filled her new cupboards with things she could cook on a gas ring, now that her whole kitchen consisted of two, and a pipe to a gas bottle.

The day had been long, and she was bone tired. The light slipped into dusk and she sat in the doorway of her new shed, and watched the sky and the sun do the melting impossible, beautiful sunset thing. It was different to watching it all drop into the sea, but instead it painted the hills with light and shadow, spilled the pink and orange across the moor and stood the small stands of trees in silhouette. Her pasta bubbled on the gas ring, and she waited, her stomach rumbling and full of butterflies at the huge leap she'd made. Dinner was ready, and she could not have been readier herself. Laughing at how much she had cooked, she set aside the extra pasta and sat on the step to eat.

To her left she could see the outline of a huge digger, which had already made a good start on the drive in, piles of boulders sat on one side. She felt her eyelids slide towards closing, and pushed herself up to go inside. A noise to her right made her jump up, sleep and tiredness forgotten. She stood, her knees bent in readiness, her eyes scanning the thickening darkness, her breath coming in hard, fast gasps. The noise came again, a whine, or a whimper, a twig snapping. She stepped towards it. Her heart thumping against her ribs.

The whimper was louder the next time. Whatever was making it, sounded as though there was pain involved. She took another step, her hand out in front of her, straining to see what was making the noise. Her hand hit something, and the whine and whimper was louder now. She felt matted fur under her fingers, ears perhaps. She stepped backwards, and a dog stepped out of the shadows. Skinny, with ribs showing through the rough, matted fur, eyes so sad it made her heart squeeze.

"Hey, you look hungry, like you haven't eaten for a month. Do you want something to eat? I have loads of pasta, let me see if I can find something to add to it to make it a bit more interesting." She grabbed the pan of cold pasta, and opened a cupboard in the shed, running her eyes over the tins, and settling on a tin of sardines. That might work. "Here you go. Try this." She mixed the pasta shapes with the sardines from the tin and put the bowl down carefully. The dog gulped down the bowl in a few mouthfuls, and looked hopefully at her. She poured some water into the bowl and watched as it was lapped up. She sat back down on the step, and waited. The dog lay down, just a few feet away, and together, in silence, and, what felt to her comfortable companionship, they contemplated the dark night that wrapped around them, a little dot of light in a wide-open moor.

The air changed, the chill seeped into her feet and hands. The first drops of rain fell, fat and fast, and she stepped inside before it got worse. The dog sat up. She took a breath in.

"Do you want to come inside?" She asked. The big eyes said yes, but nothing else moved. "Come on then." She held the door open. She watched the wariness fight with the need to be warm and dry. Warm and dry won, and the dog slipped through the door, sniffing the floor and the scant furnishings she had installed, before selecting a corner as far away from the bed as was possible, and lying down. She shrugged and went to bed, and listened to the rain on the roof, and the snoring of the dog. The noises comforted her and she found she was drifting to sleep.

Later, much later, still dark, but maybe getting light around the edges, Julia half woke up, her hand was resting on the dog's head. It was warm, and the fur was soft, and the experience, one she had felt before but not since she was a child, was a balm to her soul, and even though she was only half aware of it, she smiled as she slipped back to sleep.

4.

He had been able to help Julia get a job, when she applied to a letting agency. He owned a lot of property which he rented out. The letting agent was happy to help him and reported back that his recommendation had been absolutely the right way to go, when Julia turned out to be very good at her job. She worked hard, and was promoted, running a branch of her own only two years after she started.

Janice's illness made him realize what was important, the business he had embraced as a young man had changed. He had no need to make any more money. His properties paid him enough rent to live very comfortably. When he slipped away, without telling anyone where he was going, or what his plans were, he anticipated that his trusted business partner would step into his shoes, without missing a beat.

The last house he bought in London had belonged to Janice. He paid more than the asking price, to give the money to his daughter. He left it empty.

Once he knew that his daughter was making a new life in Cornwall he found some land, and discovered a new appreciation of the natural world. He bought some chickens, laughing as they ran around the run he had built, and cheering to himself when they laid eggs. He watched from a distance, and saw his daughter build a strong business. He was proud of her, but knew he had no right to approach her directly. It was enough to stand back, and see where she took the life she made.

When he found out about her man, and what he had done, he

was furious. There was nothing cold or resentful about this, it burned his insides and set his teeth against each other. When she cut her hair short and rolled up her sleeves, he had never been so proud of anything. He watched her build and paint and scrub, and then every day, he took himself to the beach, and drank coffee, while he watched her swim.

He knew he had been a bad man, and that he had made some very bad decisions, but if there was a God somewhere, then he had truly smiled down on the day that child was born. He had no right to be in her life, but he could watch from the side lines and feel proud of his blood running around in her veins.

He was getting old. Life had been kind and unkind in equal measure, like most lives. His body was weaker than it had been, but he had never been happier. He bought himself a puppy, and watched the little ball of hair grow. He named it Mik, the word for friend in his own language, and then laughed to find out that it was a common name for men in his adopted country. His chickens laid their eggs, and his dog ran in circles. He was given a cow, who ate the grass in his field. In the winter, he walked across the field he owned and patted his cow. In the summer he sat outside his house in the warm sun and watched the animals, he even enjoyed cleaning up after them. He used their manure to improve the soil, and took great pleasure in growing vegetables for his table. He kept his life very quiet. He had changed his name when he moved to Cornwall, but he suspected there were people who would like to know where he was. He had made his peace with the world, but perhaps the world had yet to forgive him.

He made his Will and left it with a solicitor he visited in Plymouth. He felt that he had set everything right. Every box had been ticked. All that was required was to settle back and enjoy what was left of his life.

5.

Ben pulled up next to the open gate, and climbed out. He walked into the yard, there was nowhere for him to park there, every inch seemed to be full of vans. He spotted a face he recognised in the group talking together and raised his hand in greeting.

Gemma's hair was long, tied up in a ponytail, and dark. Stray strands had escaped and straggled across her face. She pushed it behind her ears.

"Ben, over here." He shook hands with everyone in the group. "This is Ben, our local vet, very helpful. Thanks for coming out on a Saturday. Come with me, I'll show you what we found." She pulled up the mask that had fallen beneath her chin. "You might want one of these." She pushed open the door to the chicken barn, and the smell met him like a wall. He gagged, then breathed slowly out. She pulled a mask out of her pocket and passed it to him. Gratefully, he tucked the loops behind his ears. It helped, a bit.

The sight that met him made his eyes close, until he could pull himself together. There were dead chickens everywhere. The floor was covered with faeces and littered with bodies. The smell was hitting the back of his throat, and the sadness of the scene made his chest ache.

"Come outside so we can talk." Her hand held over her mouth; she went outside. "God, that's dreadful." She leaned against the low wall that ran away from the chicken shed. It looked as though she was fighting the urge to vomit.

"What happened, Gemma?" Ben breathed the fresh air, glad to be outside.

"The owner is missing. I guess they had no food or water." She pulled out a tissue and wiped her face.

"So why call me in?" He waited while he watched a decision travel across her face.

"Something went on here. I want your opinion on the animals. There's a dead cow in the other building over there, and I was hoping you could tell me more about the chickens."

"Show me the cow." They walked fast across the yard, and she pulled up the mask again. The cow was lying on its side, with a slash across her throat up to her shoulder, and a puddle of what was once blood around her, the wound, a huge flap of skin, was alive with maggots. "Shit. I need to look at the chickens again."

"Be my guest." She stepped away, and waited outside for him. He wasn't more than two minutes.

"I think some of them ruptured. Hard to tell when they've started to decompose. They may have been fed something that swelled up really fast, too quick to let them get it out, some of them have split inside, there's always mess around chickens, but that's beyond normal. Somebody gave them something that killed them. I can't know if it was on purpose or not. What happened to that cow was on purpose." He wiped his sleeve across his eyes. This was too hard. "I was up here a few weeks ago, because he was worried about the chickens, wanted me to give them a once over. They were fine." He turned away from her, embarrassed by his emotions, his anger at the waste of it all.

"OK, email me an opinion?" She bit her bottom lip. "Also, can you tell me a bit about him?"

He thought about it. "Nice guy, I liked him. Old fashioned, I suppose, but he loved the life, cared for his animals. Always paid his bill on time, that's unusual. Loved his dog. Where's the dog?"

"We didn't find any dogs." She pulled her notebook out of her pocket and checked. "No, definitely no dogs."

"He was always smart, shirt and tie, you know the kind of thing, old school. I came out last winter, it was bitter, icy on the roads, but he was worried about the dog, he'd cut his paw, and he wanted me to look at it. He'd bandaged it and sat with the dog all night." He nodded to her. "I'll send you an opinion. No charge. I liked him."

"Thanks Ben." Gemma smiled and walked back to the rest of them. "What did you call him?"

"Mr Alex."

He walked fast, wanting to put distance between himself and what he'd seen. The car made him feel better. He closed his eyes and tried to shut out the pictures in his head. His phone beeped. He took a breath and checked the messages. A message from the surgery, asked if he could see a dog, a stray. It was miles away. Couldn't be the same dog, but it was on the way back to the surgery, he'd take a look.

6.

The morning started early and brought Jamie, Callum and Joe, ready to drive the digger and move the earth and rocks. They stopped for breakfast after a couple of hours, Julia made toast and scrambled eggs, for all of them, including the dog. He stayed out of the way of the builders and the machines and after they ate, he took himself off for a walk while they went back to work. Jamie checked levels on the chain saws, and the crew spent the rest of the morning taking the tree in the middle of the main building down, while Julia and Joe pulled the branches away, stacking them out of the way. By lunchtime the pieces of tree were too big to drag away, so Joe moved them with the digger, wrapping chains around them and dragging them, until the tree was gone, and then they dug out the roots, digging around them, then pulling slowly with the heavy machine. They worked until the roots were gone, and the day was almost gone with them. Julia stood to one side, with Jamie and Callum watching Joe scraping the earth and left over roots out of the building, ready for the concrete to arrive the next day.

She waved goodbye and lit the gas under her pasta pan. The dog arrived back soon after she dished hers up, and enjoyed his. She decided to find a local vet, and check he was doing OK if he stayed for much longer. In the meantime, they were getting on OK, he had better manners than the last man she lived with, and after a quick luke-warm shower she sat in her pyjamas aching everywhere, as the sun dipped in the sky, and she found the dog edging close enough to touch. She rested her hand on the step, halfway between them, and watched him shuffle so that his head rested on the step, within an inch of her fingers. Smiling she covered the small gap, and rested her fingers gently on his head, still for a moment on the soft fur. He took a breath, and let it go, sounding like a sigh. Slowly, she stroked his ears, watching the golden hairs in the glow of the lamplight. He moved closer, slowly, until his warm body rested against hers, leaning his shoulder into her, with her arm draped over his back. She watched his tongue lolling out, and felt the weight of him, and it made her smile.

Another night slept with a dog in the shed, surprised by how wonderful it felt when he settled down next to the bed.

Another night, slept as though she had been shot, while her body recovered from the work, but she knew she would get stronger, with every day that passed.

Lying in the dark, she felt the excitement of her new life, and the exhaustion of getting there, and the simple happiness of having a dog in her life, who liked pasta for dinner, and eggs and toast for breakfast. Every day stretched her muscles and her smile, and she changed as much as the land and the buildings.

When the first weekend arrived, she had never been so glad. Early on Saturday morning, she pulled on her wet suit, and climbed into the land rover.

"Dog. Come on boy." She watched him take a look and decide to go with it. He jumped in, and sat in the front seat next to her. She pulled the door shut and set off, through empty streets. Nobody was up yet. She reached the beach before six, and called the dog to cross the sand with her, pulling up the zip on her wet suit. Following her into the surf, he jumped back from the water, but seeing her slip in up to her waist, he followed her, and brought himself level with her, his paws working hard to swim in the cold crisp water. She smiled and swam with him, laughing at the way he splashed through the water, and kept his head and ears high and dry. She turned towards the beach and he came with her, laughing when he found the sand under his feet again, and barked. Wagging his tail and shaking the water from his fur. He followed her to the shower, and stood patiently while she rinsed the salt out of her hair and his fur.

They walked slowly back to the car, and she dried him with the towel she had brought with her. She put a dry one on the seat, and let him in to the car. He curled up on it and was asleep before she pulled out of the car park. She had made an order online, and collected her shopping. The dog slept on.

Her phone rang as she drove through her gate. "Hello?"

"Hi. You left a message for me, I'm Ben Winton, the Vet." He sounded distracted, but friendly.

"Oh, thank you, for calling back I mean. I found a dog, he was very hungry and tired, and he's, well, sort of moved in. I thought perhaps I should get him checked, to see if he needs anything, except food and sleep." She pulled up the handbrake, and stroked the silky fur, which looked and smelled much better after swimming.

"Where are you? Your message said you were on the moor?"

"I'm about three miles from Blisland, do you know it?" She pushed the door open and looked out across her land.

"Yes. I must be not far from you then. I just visited a farm not far from there. What's the address?" She told him. "Hugo's old place?"

"Yes. You know Hugo?"

"I do. I'm five minutes away. I'll pop in and meet your dog. I'm curious to see what you're doing with the place." He hung up and she pulled her shopping bags out of the back of the land rover, and carried them into the shed.

"Hello sleepy head." The dog hopped down out of the door she had left open. She stroked his soft head. "You're having a visitor in a minute." His tongue lolled and he gave her a lopsided look. She poured fresh water for him and unpacked the shopping.

It was the first day in a while that she had truly to herself, and sitting on the step to her shed, stroking silky soft ears in the sunshine seemed a really good way to spend it. Her body was glad of the break, and everything about her was grateful for the good weather, and for the dog. She pushed up from the step when she saw a head of dark hair climbing up from the gate. She watched him getting closer. He was dressed in an old fleece which had seen better days and dark trousers which were more mud than any fabric.

"Hi." She called out. "Thanks for this." He covered the ground fast, and held his hand out in front of him.

"Ben. Hi, I'm the vet." He smiled and it changed his face, he had looked almost sullen, definitely fed up, but now he twinkled at her.

"Julia. This is the dog. He's eating and drinking OK, but he was so skinny and tired I was worried I should just check." She watched him kneel on the grass in front of the dog. His hand reached in a pocket and came out with a biscuit.

"Here you go. Let's have a look. He looks good. A bit on the skinny side, a few weeks of proper eating will fix that, his eyes and ears look fine. He looks like a dog over on a farm I do some work at, they're probably related." He stroked the dog, checking the pad on his front left paw, where a thick scar raised from the skin. "What are you calling him?"

"Dog, at the moment. If he stays on, I'll think up a name." Julia smiled at the two of them sitting on the grass. "Do you want a coffee?"

"Thanks, that would be good." She disappeared into the shed and put the kettle on. "So, what are you doing here?"

"I'm fixing it." She watched him over the rim of her cup, then her eyes drifted to the view over his shoulder. "Look at it. The view alone makes all this worthwhile. I think I can make the houses pretty amazing too. Which is why I'm living in a shed, with a dog who has no name, and pulling rocks and mud and lumps of tree all over the place." She laughed, low and quiet in the back of her throat, turning her hands to look at the scratches and bruises she had earned in her first week as a labourer.

"Where were you before?" His eyes were deep brown, and he could have looked dark and brooding, if he stopped smiling for a minute.

"Constantine Bay. I ran a holiday let business there. I saw this place, and I made a decision." She felt a wet nose pushing her hand, and smiled down at him. "So, he's OK, nothing to worry about?"

"You're doing a good job with him. He's still underweight, by the look of him, but there's nothing wrong with him that good food and a warm home won't fix. I need to scan him to see if he's chipped, someone might be looking for him." She watched him pull out a hand-held scanner and run it over the dog's coat. She felt her shoulders hunch, surprised how much she would miss the dog if he were to be taken away from her. A beep answered the question. "He is chipped. Hang on and I'll have a look at where he was registered."

He walked away, leaving her feeling bereft, sitting on the step, her arm around the dog, her coffee forgotten, wishing she had never called the vet, telling herself that someone was missing this dog, and worried about him. She had no claim on him, except that him being with her felt right. She watched the vet walk back from his car.

She looked so sad. He had to check, even though he was sure, absolutely certain it was the same dog. The code on the scanner confirmed it. He walked back, not really knowing how much he should tell her.

"Hi. OK. The chip says I was right, he is registered to a farm about ten miles away, he's had a long journey to find you." He smiled. "Look, I was called out to the farm, the owner had gone missing, and they needed to sort out the animals. The dog was missing. There's no family I know of. I'll check, but I suspect if you want him, he's yours." Her face split into a huge smile.

"Oh, wow. Thank you. D'you hear that, Dog?" She stroked his head, and he lifted his eyes to look at her face, snaking a wet tongue out to slap across her cheek. "Yuk. Thanks, dog." She rubbed his ears. "Thank you so much Ben. I hadn't realized how much I wanted him to stay."

"His name is, was I suppose, Mick." He chuckled to himself. The dog sat upright at his name. "I don't know why. He was loved, in case you were thinking he ran away because he had a bad life. I recognized the scar on his front paw. I was called out when he cut his foot, he was curled up on the sofa, with a blanket around him, and a bandage the size of a football on this leg." He sat down on the step next to her, and stroked the dog. "I'll talk to the chip people and let them know he's been rehomed."

"Mick." She shook her head. The dog wiggled forward, resting his chin on her knee. "OK. Mick it is." She rested her hand down on his neck. "What happened to his owner?"

"I don't know." He shrugged. "When do you think you'll be moving in?" He nodded towards the building where the work was in progress.

"Before the cold weather comes, I hope. I don't want to be in the shed then." Her eyes drifted to the view, and she took a breath. "He must have been frightened then, to run away. If the owner went away without him."

"Yeah. I guess." They sat together, watching the clouds puff across the wide blue sky. "I've lived near here all my life, and I don't appreciate it enough. You're right, this view is worth looking at." He nodded, and passed her his empty cup. "Thank you. Nice to have a cuppa. It's been a long day." He pushed his hair off his face, rubbed his other hand over the dog's back. He pushed himself to his feet. "Can I pop by in a few weeks? See how far you've got with the house?"

"Of course. I'm here most of the time." She waved as he walked away, and carried the cups back in.

7.

"Mickey boy? Let's go for a walk." She pushed the door of the shed closed and set off towards the woods. It was uphill and the ground was uneven, but getting up there meant that she could sit down and see for miles. Mick sat next to her for a while, then he fell asleep. She could see the lane from there, and watched a land rover pass by. To the right, beyond her fence, were more fields, and then another bit of woodland. To the left was her land, and the buildings. Then the lane. It was quiet and peaceful, except for Mick's snoring.

A car pulled up in the lane. She watched the driver, and stilled. She breathed, and rested her hand on the dog's chest, feeling him rise and fall with her. A man walked slowly to the gate. Her gate, she realized. He looked out of place, too much city, not enough country. His gaze travelled across her land, passing over her and the dog, without pausing. She waited, and drew her breath carefully, until he seemed satisfied and climbed back into his car and drove away. For no reason that she could see, he had unsettled her. Huffing a breath out, she patted the dog and got to her feet, and walked up the hill and into the woods, while he trotted behind her.

The car slowed, and pulled in again, further down the lane, and he got out. He pushed the door slowly, carefully. He moved slowly back to the fence line, and between the branches. He had a good view of the buildings, and across the lower half of the land. He wasn't sure if she'd seen him. He wanted a closer look, but he didn't want to scare her. It would have to wait until later. He took a breath and let it out again. This was more complicated than he had thought. The land was on a slope, and there were areas which were hard to see. He would drive around and see if he could get into the woodland. That was the best way, then he could see, and still be hidden within the trees.

She circled around the woodland, and then back down towards the buildings. Her stomach grumbled, reminding her that it would be time to eat soon. The clouds scudding across the sky warned of changing weather. The air was still warm and smelled of the pine trees and the soft earth. She leaned a hand against the bark of a tree, and she reminded herself that this was her land, and these were her trees.

A noise behind them brought the dog's ears up, and sent him bounding between the trees, bouncing on the soft springy grass and ferns. She watched his tail rise and fall, then smiled when he padded back towards her, looking pleased with himself.

He parked up and pushed his arms into a waterproof jacket, slipping out of the car and dragging his backpack onto his shoulders, before locking up. His strong all-weather boots made the hike easy, following the line of the fence, for ten minutes before turning towards the trees he could see. He had to cross another field and a shallow stream before climbing a hill to find the edge of the woodland, and the fence that he climbed to take him onto her land. The rain started when he was climbing the hill, and a few minutes later he reached the protection of the trees, where the water dripped from the leaves and the pine needles and he walked, quiet through the silent trees.

Back at the shed, she made an omelette for herself, and fed the dog a bowl of pasta. They sat on the step, protected from the rain, and watching the evening light, and the clouds. Her body ached, new muscles she hadn't been aware she owned hurt. She felt more comfortable after her walk, but she needed to sleep soon.

The rain seemed to be settled in for the night, so she shrugged her shoulders, closed the door, and carried a book to her bed, settling herself against the pillows and reading a few pages before her eyes dipped in longer and longer blinks. Her head dropped and the book fell forward. The dog curled comfortably on the floor next to her bed and they slept.

He watched the light in the shed as the land around it faded into the darkness. The rain fell, and dripped across his eyes and off his chin, and still he stood, and still the rain fell. Later, when he returned to his car, he was almost surprised to find that he was wet, right through to his underwear.

8.

"Ben?" Her voice was professional, cool. "I got your opinion. Thanks for sending it through. I've had the contents of the chickens' stomachs tested, and it seems you were right. They were fed an industrial foam product. It swells when it gets wet. Very nasty."

"Poor things. Are you OK, Gemma?" He cradled the phone between his shoulder and his jaw. "This must be difficult for you."

"Thanks Ben. Honestly, this is a weird one. I haven't seen anything like this before." She huffed. "Just wanted to let you know you were right."

"What do you think it means?" He stopped in front of a bank of cages, where two dogs were recovering from surgery.

"I don't know. I wish I did. Thanks Ben. Got to go." He could hear people talking in the background, before the phone cut off.

Gemma took a breath, all the way down to her boots, rubbed her hands together and opened the folder in front of her. The pile of papers inside, lists and reports and statements, she spread out across the desk. Her fingers skittered across them, as though she could extract some information by touch, which reading and checking and double testing each item on each page had not yet given her.

She pushed back in her seat. The man had lived on his farm for less than ten years. Before that, there was no record of him. Nobody had anything bad to say about him. That in itself was a bit odd. Most people who had lived somewhere for a few years had managed to annoy someone. It was nowhere nearly enough. It looked as though someone had searched his house, or maybe he was just messy.

In the open plan office around her, phones rang, and voices murmured, but she blocked them out, her focus sharpening into the details, and the conversations she had had with people through the investigation so far. There was something that she was missing, of that she was certain. The reason, and she was fully aware of the resentment it caused sometimes, that she had gained promotion at a younger age, was this commitment to a case, and her ferocious attention to detail. Her notes joined the file on her desk as she checked through them. There it was, the niggling thin stray thought that had been left to wander, unchecked. Her hand reached for the phone again and she rang the vet back.

"Hi Ben, sorry to bother you again. Can you just run over one more thing?" He made a noise, somewhere between agreement and irritation. "The dog, you said there was a dog missing from the crime scene."

"Oh, yes. He's fine, he turned up, tired and hungry, perhaps he ran off, when Mr Alex went missing, but he's found a new home, and he's settled in well." She could hear he was smiling, glad that the dog was happy.

"Right. While that is great news for the dog, my focus is more on the owner." She cut back on the sarcasm. "Sorry, tough day. If this dog ran off, scared perhaps, is it possible he might recognise and react to a suspect?"

"It depends on what he saw. He might have just found himself alone, and been scared by that, I have no way of knowing."

The vet was right. "Ok. Thanks, maybe I'm just clutching at straws. I'll let you get on, thanks Ben."

So, what did she know about this man, he spoke perfect English, with a slight accent, but nobody could pinpoint where his accent was from. There was a general feeling that he was from eastern Europe, but not from any evidence. He was a farmer, on a smallholding, clearly not making much of a living, but not spending much either, he was happy, it seemed, so why did he up and disappear. His passport, which had been unearthed, inside a locked box, behind a row of books. Hidden? Perhaps, or put away safely? It gave his name as Alexander Roscoff, and his nationality as Lithuanian. She was fairly sure it was a fake. There were no other documents. He clearly drove a car but she had found no driving licence. There were no credit cards, some cash, but not loads. He almost didn't exist.

She pushed back from her desk, frustrated by how much she knew was missing. This man loved his animals, called out the vet regularly, and paid on time. He sat up all night with his dog. Someone killed his animals in a brutal, cruel, vicious way. To force the man to tell them something? To punish him for something? To hurt him? Did he leave of his own accord? Was he taken?

9.

The huge wooden triangles were hauled up and set along the length of the walls. Julia helped to connect the chains and pulled against the weight, along with Joe, to winch them up. They would be supporting her roof, so she accepted that her muscles would burn and strain in the effort. Each day brought new surprises and moved her house closer to completion. She was only a few days away from having a roof, and maybe a week or two away from having windows, and a door. She was a long way from moving in, but every step took her closer. The team of builders who had started by putting up with her, had become friends, and accepted her, she felt, if not as one of them, then at least not as a liability.

"Hey, Jules?" She turned towards the voice. Joe was waving at her. "There's a guy here looking for you." She waved back, and walked towards him. As she crossed the grass, the gate came into view, and a man stood waiting. He wore a dark blue shirt, and jeans. His hair was thick, cut short at the sides, but longer on top, with wavy curls.

"Hi. Are you from the Planning Department? I didn't realize we had an appointment." She reached the gate, and looked at a face that she thought looked familiar.

"No. No, I'm not from…. Um, I need to talk to you, just five minutes." His accent clipped his words.

"I don't have any money to buy anything, I'm in the middle of a building project, and it's eating all my money." She laughed, and turned away.

"No, it's not about that. Please, just five minutes." His eyes locked hers. She felt sure that she had met him before.

"A short story. In 1987, my father left our home, to work for a man, ending up in this country. The man he worked for, was a gangster. My father was a fool, he stole. I was nearly three, and my sister had just been born. The gangster sent two men to our home, to grab me, to force my father to tell the truth, I think. I was with my Aunt, but my baby sister was in the house, and they took her. By the time they brought her here, my father had died." He shrugged. "An over enthusiastic beating from his colleagues. In any case, the gangster was stuck with a baby. His girlfriend at the time, a girl called Janice, took care of the baby, and decided to leave him, change her name and take the child on as her own." He paid close attention to her reaction. "Does it make sense so far?" She nodded.

"The baby was you. I am your brother." He stood so still it was hard to know what she should do.

"I. No, you made a mistake. I am so sorry that you lost your sister, but it's not me." She gulped breath.

"I know it's a lot to take in. I've known most of it since I was a child. We can do a DNA test if you want. Look at my face. We are brother and sister. We look alike. You are very like our mother." He reached out his hand towards her.

"You're telling me my Mother was with some violent gangster? That's not true. You've made a mistake." Her voice shook with emotion. "You can't just walk in here and tell someone stuff like this."

"I know. I get it. So, I want to leave you to think about it. I'll leave you my number, and I'll be in touch once you've had some time. I didn't want to upset you. I came before, but you were on your own, so I waited until you had people here, so that you would feel safe. I am your big brother. I want you to feel safe. OK?" He stepped back from the gate, and smiled, climbing into his car.

She closed her eyes, trying to steady the breath roaring through her brain. His car pulled away from the gate. He was right, that they looked alike. The rest had to be rubbish though. He had wrong footed her. This had to be some sort of scam. Shaking her head, she pushed herself away from the gate and walked back up the hill. This was going to take some thinking about, to work out what he was after.

She chewed her lip, pushing his visit down into her thoughts. They had two more hours of work time and she needed to concentrate to make herself useful. Better to push her muscles and her back than to let her mind run free.

"You OK Julia?" Joe creased his forehead. "You've been quiet this afternoon."

"I would have thought you would be grateful for the peace." She pushed a smile. "I'm OK. Just tired. See you tomorrow."

She watched them climb into the van and drive away, and sat on the grass, her arm nudged by Mick as he sat down next to her. "Hello, Mickey boy. Are you thinking it might be time for some dinner?" She ruffled his fur, leaning into the warmth of his shoulder. Something about the warmth of him, the weight of his body and his solid feel made her crumble inside. Big fat tears ran down her face. She missed her Mum, and it was hard to hear someone say that she, the woman who had cared for her, and been there all through growing up and beyond wasn't really her Mum, especially now that there was no way for her to check. It felt as though she had been disloyal even listening to the man who claimed he was her brother. The dog shifted his weight, and licked her hand. She leaned back, and swiped her hand across her face. Time to make something to eat. She patted the soft head, and climbed back up the hill.

Her phone rang later while she ate, and she was pleased to see Lou's name come up.

"Hey." Julia pushed her plate away.

"Hello. How was your day?"

"Um, a bit weird. How about yours?" Why was she not able to just tell her friend about this?

"I was offered a day and a half at the hotel I went to see today. They want to offer yoga and relaxation. Should be good, and all through the winter too. I wanted to thank you, for being so supportive, knowing I had you behind me made me, sort of, braver." She took a breath. "If you're not busy tonight, how about I bring a bottle of wine to yours, I'd love to meet your new dog."

"Honestly, Lou, that would be so lovely. I'm feeling a bit wobbly, I could use a chat."

"I'll be there in a bit. Don't worry about food, I ate already. See you soon."

"That's some weird bananas." Lou's eyes were open wide. She ate a crisp, and sipped her wine. "It's such a bizarre story. Do you believe him?"

"I don't want to. I know my Mum always said she had changed her name, because my dad had been unkind to her. I thought he might have even been aggressive, or perhaps a drunk, when I was growing up. She never told me anything else. I can't ask her. She can't defend herself from what he's saying. I feel like I should protect her, but I have no defence." Julia rested her head on her hand.

"Love, you can't. Even if it's true, it doesn't change how much she loved you. It might not even be true. If it is, maybe it means she loved you even more. At the end of it, all of it, there is only love, or lack of." She reached for Julia's hands. "You didn't lack. She loved you."

Julia wiped a tear, as it slipped away from her lashes. "I loved her too, and I miss her. Sometimes I feel like she's still around. I think, Mum would like that, or I've got to remember to tell Mum about this. I feel, adrift, without her."

"I know. I felt like that when my dad passed away. I used to buy those horrible sausages that he liked, I hated the things but I kept buying them because he would be round for his dinner every Thursday. I couldn't stop." She laughed, a little shaky noise.

"Do you still buy them?" Julia pushed her hair back and sniffed.

"Yeah, I got used to them, I sort of like them." She sipped her wine.

"I'm not coming to dinner with you on a Thursday." They both laughed. Lou stood up and wrapped her arms around her friend.

10.

June 2018

The excitement she should be feeling, with the roof on her new home, and work starting on the windows was missing. Her mind questioned everything, every memory she had held close to her heart. Her whole relationship with her mother called into question, by a man who looked so familiar, because, when she looked in his face, she saw her own.

Her Mum had been so sweet, when she was at school, her friends used to love coming to her house, because her Mum made them so welcome, and was so much fun. The nights she had spent snuggled on the sofa with her Mum, watching movies, and laughing at silly jokes together. They had argued, of course they had, over too much make up, when Julia was a teenager, too short skirts, normal teenage stuff. They had made up fast, and laughed about it later, over tea and biscuits. Now Julia's memories were tinged with questions over whether it had been real, or had it been pretended all her life? Julia had an image of her Mum being sweet and kind. Had she really been going out with a gangster? The whole idea was ridiculous, but if she accepted that the man had been her brother, then at least some of the rest of his story had to be true. It felt as though everything had shifted. She felt angry, that she had been lied to, that she felt so completely wrong footed, and if it was true, that she had been snatched from her mother when she was a baby.

The dog sat next to her, on the hard, concrete base that would be the floor to her house, under her new roof. The rain started to fall softly on the new tiles, and she tipped her head back to look at the underneath of the roof. In the shadow, the rafters were beautiful, strong, and structural. She closed her eyes.

"Mickey boy. Does it matter, do you think, if she wasn't my biological mum? I guess you don't know your Mum at all, do you?" He nuzzled his face into her neck. "Maybe that's the answer. I love you too, you big, fluffy idiot." She laughed, her face buried in his fur, and her arms around his neck. "Come on. We'll have a quick walk before we settle down for the night." They followed the wall of the house, and turned left, climbing to the trees, then turning right to make a circle back to the shed. The dog ran ahead, bouncing through the long grass, dancing and jumping.

On the road, he stood, binoculars trained on her, following their progress back to the shed. Carefully climbing back into his car, and closing the door slowly, he leaned back against the seat, letting out a long breath. His eyes stung, he had to hold himself tight, his whole life had been leading to this. He knew that he could frighten her off, so easily, and he needed her, he had to bring her to him, pull her into the family. Since he was a small boy, he had known that he must find her, but events had overtaken him, and he had to step carefully. But quickly, so quickly. The familiar dull thud of pain in his temple, spoke of stress and his responsibility, the weight he carried, crushing his head, pushing it down into his neck so he struggled to breathe. His fingers tensed, curling into his fists. He forced himself to pull in air, and push it out. To concentrate on holding everything inside him, together, until he could tie all the ends up, then he would have done what was needed, and his sister, sitting over the other side of the field, in a shed, was the key.

The morning sent him looking for breakfast, and he found a small place with wipe-clean furniture, where he ordered food, pushing it around the cardboard it arrived in. His stomach growled and burned with acid. He yearned for proper food. He had eaten enough of this fried rubbish to last his whole life.

The phone in his pocket vibrated, and a large part of him was glad to push the plastic food away from him. The number made him sit up straighter.

Gemma collected her take away coffee, her mind running in circles over the information she had committed to memory, everything relating to the case. This was the way she worked, sinking herself into the information, finding the part that stood out, the piece that jarred with the rest. The coffee here was better than at the station, and she found walking helped her brain work. It sometimes shook something loose, and she surely needed some help with this one. A sip, reassured her that the coffee was hitting its usual standard.

She recognised the man behind the counter, and one of the two customers, Jim. She had arrested his son the year before, after a spate of burglaries. The other man was a stranger. He spoke fast, quietly, and not in English, on his phone. She waited until her had finished his call, for no reason except that he was exactly what she was looking for. He was out of place.

He finished his call, and she watched, he pushed his food further away across the table. His face was handsome, but he looked unhappy, his eyes were distracted, his fingers were restless.

"Hi. Sorry to bother you, I couldn't help overhearing. Was that Albanian you were speaking?" She stepped across the space to his table.

"You speak the language?" His eyes, now they were focused on her, were very intense.

"No." She laughed. It sounded fake inside her head. "I've been listening to some recordings lately, for work, and I thought I recognized some of the sounds, words, I don't know. Sorry." She shook her head, as though she was surprised by herself. "I'm Gemma Wilton, Detective Sergeant." She watched for it. It was there, the tiny flicker, he was quick, but she was waiting to see it, so she caught it, before he hid it. She breathed out the air she had been holding, and smiled at him. "If I'd met you before, I could have asked for your help. It's strange, I'd never met anyone from Albania a week ago." She sat down at his table, uninvited.

"Was there something that you wanted?" He tipped his head, and stared at her.

"This is a small town. My job, or at least, one of them, is to notice things which are out of the ordinary. Things that stand out. What do you do?" She rested her elbow on the shiny plastic table.

"I don't do anything at the moment, I am on holiday. I will go home soon. But I am enjoying your Cornwall countryside." He smiled, it looked as though his face was surprised by it.

"Are you, by any chance, visiting family here?" She smiled, her voice light.

"I am here on holiday. I read, when I was learning English, a book about English counties. I wanted to come here, ever since." He watched her carefully.

"Ah. Right. Would you, I wonder be prepared to help, if, say, I needed someone to translate for me, or something?" She smiled.

"If I'm still here. I only have a week before I have to go home." He nodded, trying to end the conversation.

"So, can I take your number, your name?" She pulled out her phone, and he told her the number. "And, your name?"

"Florian." He pushed up from the chair. "Now if you will excuse me, I am meeting someone shortly."

"Ah, well, I wouldn't want to hold you up, if you're off on a hot date. Thank you, Florian." She keyed in his name, and pressed the call icon. His phone rang. "Oops. Silly me." She smiled, and stepped towards the door, slipping her phone into her pocket, and puling the door open, sipping her coffee, walking quickly to her car. She slid into the driver's seat, and waited.

Sipping slowly, she waited some more, watched him leave, and climb into his own car, further down the road. Slowly and carefully, she pulled out and followed him, allowing one, and then another car to pull out between them.

He drove out of the town, and up onto the moor. The landscape grew less manicured, less managed, wilder. She had to balance, keeping him in sight, but not getting too close. It was harder without the traffic to hide in.

He wound his way through the lanes. When he stopped, she was lucky to spot that he had pulled in, so that she could stop in a passing place. She waited, she thought she was probably out of his sight line, unless he knew that she was following him, and was watching for her.

She was too far away to see for sure that he was still in the car. If she got out of her car, he could drive off and would lose her. He could have got out before she pulled up. This is why she should have called it in, not gone off on her own, following her instincts was good, but now she had put herself in a stupid position.

Cursing under her breath, she tucked her phone into her pocket and zipped up her waterproof, slipping out of the car as the first drops of rain fell heavily out of the sky. Pulling her hood up would keep her dry and perhaps change how she looked a little. She pushed her keys and her hands into the pockets and walked towards his parked car, her breath came a little faster, and her heart sounded loud in her ears. The car was empty. She sighed, this was why she spent most of her time behind a desk, thinking.

11.

June 2018

Ben loaded his bag and his wellies into the back of his car, and slipped his feet into trainers, counting the payment and slipping it into his folder. He drove away, and chewed his lip over the question that had been buzzing around his head like an angry bee, for days. He liked her, for the first time in a very long time, he had met a new woman, and he wanted to see her again. He had stayed away, and now he wished he had been there before now. He pulled into the gap by her gate. The rain was falling steadily and his windscreen blurred with the water as soon as the wipers stopped. He scrolled to her number and dialled, before he could talk himself out of it again.

"Hello, Julia, it's Ben." He smiled in the quiet of the car, wondering if he sounded as close to fifteen as he felt.

"Hey Ben, how are you?"

"All good, thank you. I wondered if you were at home, I've just come away from a job up the road from you, and I thought, if you were free, I could pop in and see you." He rubbed his thumb over his fingers.

"That would be lovely. I'll put the kettle on. How far away are you?"

"I'm parked by your gate." A laugh bubbled up through his chest.

"You should be here by the time it's boiled then." She heard the laugh in his voice, and laughed too.

He climbed out of the car, and locked up, before he slipped the gate open, and closed again, and climbed up the hill, with rain pelting down on his head,

She was waiting on the step, with the dog. He walked carefully to her, his breath coming faster, and not just because he had walked across the field.

"Hi. Sorry. this was a bit last minute." He ruffled the dog's ears.

"I'm glad you phoned. Come in, out of the rain. I have a chair, Mick and I take turns, but as you are the guest you can have it." She laughed, and poured the coffees.

"How have you been?" He watched her walk back with the cups.

"It's been interesting. The house is coming along, I have a roof, nearly, and, it seems, I have a brother, that I didn't know about." She clapped her hand over her mouth. "Sorry, I don't know why I told you that, it's been running around in my head."

"What he just turned up?" Ben shook his head. "That must be weird."

"I know, he offered to have a DNA test, and everything, but to be honest, he looks like me. I'll do the tests, but I believe him." She sipped her tea.

"It'll be strange to get to know him now, when you're both grown up." He shrugged, perhaps she didn't want to talk about this too much. "How's our Mick, here?" The dog edged closer and accepted the attention.

"He's OK, gaining weight, getting fitter, swimming further. We walk every day, together, and he wanders around during the day, staying out of the way of the builders. I think he's settled in, seems happy."

"That's good news. So, you have a healthy dog, and a new brother. Are you interested in dinner at some point? I mean with me." He coughed, and cleared his throat. "Sorry, that came out wrong, I mean, would you like to come out for something to eat with me, if you are free one evening?"

"That would be lovely, I'd like that." She smiled at him over her cup.

"Really? Great. When would you like to go out?" He sat forward on his chair.

"How about Friday? I won't have to get up early the next day and drag rocks around then. During the week I generally eat early and sleep early."

"That would be really good. I'll pick you up. Is that OK?" She nodded.

"I was going to take the dog for a walk, do you want to come along, it looks as though the rain has taken a break." He took a drink from his cup, and zipped up his jacket. The dog knew exactly what was planned and he bounced around them. Together they left the shed, and chatted, watching the dog zig-zagging over the grass, she showed him the progress on her house, and then they turned to climb the hill together.

Hidden by the treeline, Florian watched Ben arrive, and then saw the pair walk towards him, silently he turned away, and made his way through the trees, and back to his car. They might not come into the woods, but there was no sense in taking chances. He could hear their voices and the sharp excited barks from the dog, drifting across the woodland, as he made his way across the wet grass. He had no idea who the man was, but he knew this was a distraction for her, this man was after his sister, and he had no time for her to be getting busy elsewhere.

12.

"Gemma?" He took a slow breath, this was a call he had thought about for hours, which rankled even more, because he never second guessed himself. "Hi, It's Ben. I have a question, and it might be just a bit of paranoia, or something, but I was thinking about the farm you asked me to come out to, my client, Mr Alex, he was eastern European." There was a non-committal noise on the other end of the phone. "You remember I told you about the dog, who turned up and was adopted by a girl who has a place on the moor? Well, I saw her yesterday, and she told me that a brother she has never met or known of, turned up, out of the blue and he's Albanian. He has a story about her being abducted and brought over here as a baby. She believes him, but they are going to do blood tests. I just wondered if it might be connected."

"Because of the dog?" She asked. "Or because of the eastern European connection?"

"I don't know really. It just seems to have all happened at once, and she seems to be in the middle of it somehow." He shrugged.

"OK. Did you get a name for him?"

"The dog or the brother?" He laughed, but there was no humour. "Sorry, Florian, the brother is called Florian, and the dog is called Mick."

"Oh, well, there is a coincidence. I'm not sure I really believe in those. Where does this girl live?"

"Off Haymaker Lane. Well, off, off. Hugo's old place."

"Did you say the dog was called Mick? That's unusual."

"Yeah, I guess, but I treated a cocker spaniel yesterday called Dave, so perhaps it's a thing." He felt better now he had told someone. Gemma was a steadying influence on him. She was smart, really good at her job, and calm. "Thanks for listening to me Gemma, I was in two minds whether to ring you at all."

"I'm glad you did. I'll take a drive out to see this girl, what's her name?" He could hear her shifting papers around.

"Julia." He liked the sound of her name in his mouth.

"OK. I'll have a chat with her. Thanks for letting me know. Bye." She hung up, and he slipped the phone into his pocket. He had a full clinic to get through and then a list of call outs. It was going to be a busy day.

He opened the boot of his car and pulled out his bag, there were boxes of gloves and he reminded himself to put another box in before he left the surgery. He pushed the boot closed and searched in his pocket for the surgery keys, zapping the car with the remote as he walked towards the shop front where he worked. The metal grill over the windows opened slowly, after he turned the key and he ducked underneath to unlock the front door. He had enough time, he imagined, to make a coffee, and maybe drink half of it, before the first patients arrived.

Outside, through the glass, he could see people passing by, it was the quiet end of the high street, and even the busy end was hardly Piccadilly Circus, but there were people up and down, and cars parked. He leaned against the counter and sipped his drink, watching people doing their own things, oblivious to him. He thought about Julia and how she looked when she laughed and how she made him feel when she turned her face to him, to ask him his opinion, or tell him hers. He wanted to see more of her, and that in itself was strange for him. There had been lots of dates, short lived relationships, since he had come back from University, but nobody had made him feel like this, no one had made him think of them as a possible future, beyond a happy, but maybe a bit meaningless, tumble. He smiled to himself at the expression, his father's. He had thought that he would spend his life going from one tumble to another without anything of any real substance, and had certainly not wanted anything else since Diana, who he had imagined was forever, and turned out not to be. He closed his eyes, wishing he hadn't thought of Diana at all. It was time to move on. His coffee was getting cold, and he could hear Tasha, his nurse, grinding her gears as she parked outside.

13.

June 2018

"Hello. Hello?" Gemma had climbed over the gate, and was trying to catch the attention of the building crew. A big guy spotted her waving and came over. "Hi, I'm Gemma, looking for Julia?"

"She's over there." He pointed to a wooden shed. "Said she'd make tea." He smiled widely at her and walked away.

Gemma looked around her as she crossed the field, the big machinery worried her, and fascinated her in equal measure. She skirted a little wider than strictly necessary to stay away from it.

"Hello? Hi, I'm looking for Julia." The woman, who was carrying cups of tea stopped on the step.

"I'm Julia. Are you from Building Control?"

"No, I'm a police officer, I'm investigating a possible missing person, and I need to have a chat with you, nothing to worry about, just tying up a few loose ends." Gemma watched a few expressions cross Julia's face. Surprise, concern, acceptance.

"OK, let me give these to the guys and then we can sit down, would you like a cuppa?" Gemma nodded, and waited while the teas were delivered. They sat down in the little shed and Julia passed a cup over. "So how can I help?"

"A couple of things, first of all, I hear you adopted a dog recently. He previously belonged to the man who went missing." Gemma watched her response.

"Oh, yes that's strange. The dog just turned up here, tired and hungry, so I fed him and he sort of moved in. He's a lovely dog, and it's good to have some company up here. Otherwise, it's just me." She took a sip. "Did you want to see him? He's mooching around somewhere here."

"No, that's fine. I wanted to know about something else too. The man who owned the dog, was originally Albanian, or Lithuanian as far as I can work out. I met another Albanian man this week too, and it turns out he is over here to find his long-lost sister. You." She leaned forwards. "I can't help thinking that there has to be a connection."

"Florian?" Gemma nodded. "He came up here a few days ago, I had no clue, and to start with I was quite unhappy, if I believed him then it meant my Mum had lied to me, and maybe even knew I'd been abducted. I was angry about it, and, well, unsettled by it. We are doing tests, but, honestly, he looks like me." Julia sat back, she had hunched over while she spoke, and it was uncomfortable.

"I can see the resemblance, now you mention it. You have very similar eyes." Gemma pulled a photo out of her folder. "Do you recognize this man?" Julia took the picture, and looked at it.

"Yes. I've seen him before, I used to see him most days, when I swam every day at Constantine beach, I used to live not far from there, he would be there most mornings, sometimes in the coffee place, or just sitting on the beach. I don't know his name, I don't think I ever spoke to him, more than to pass the time." She handed the picture back. "Is he the man who owned Mick? Oh yes, that's right, he had a dog with him at the beach sometimes. I had forgotten."

"Yes. His name was Alex." Gemma tucked the picture away. "I would like to take a swab from you, if that's OK?"

"For what?" Julia's eyes creased up in confusion.

"I am taking swabs from everyone who is in any way connected to this, it's a way to keep tabs, especially if you are part of a family, which is unknown to you. Very few people seem to have known anything about Alex, he kept himself to himself, so if anyone recognizes him, I need to make sure that your DNA is nowhere to be found at his home. I presume you never went to his home?"

"No, like I said he was just at the beach." Julia shrugged. "OK, take the swab."

"Thank you." Gemma pulled a long cotton bud out of a sealed test tube and passed it to Julia. "Just run it up and down on the inside of your cheek." She watched and waited, then held out the test tube to let Julia put it back in, before she fastened the lid tightly. "Look, it's not for me to advise you, but be careful with Florian. It's a lot to take in, just give yourself time to get used to it, before you dive head first into being happy families." She shrugged, tucking her folder under her arm. "Thanks for the tea."

"You're welcome." Julia stood up to watch her go, crossing the field in the bright sunlight, glittering after all the rain. Her back ached and her shoulders felt stretched beyond being useful ever again, but the crew were standing up, ready to go back to work, and she had a place there, and work to do.

When the guys packed up for the day, she went looking for Mick. He stayed away when they were busy, but she usually expected to see him trotting back to the shed, hoping for dinner, when the vans pulled out. When she called and he still was nowhere to be seen, she was concerned, and walked up towards the woods, to find him. Calling all the way, and walking faster, her voice rising when she couldn't see him, she walked into the woodland, in the shade, and saw him almost at once. He was lying under a tree, panting, and he had been sick. She ran her hand over his soft head.

"Poor boy. OK darling, hang on, I'll phone the vet and we'll get you fixed up." She dialled Ben's mobile. "Ben? Can you help me?

It's Mick. He's lying in the woods, he's been sick, he's panting, he can't get up."

"Julia. I'm on my way, I'm about ten minutes from you. Keep talking to him." The phone went dead, and she sat on the soft springy grass stroking the dog's head.

"You're such a good boy. Don't worry, Ben's on the way, he'll know what to do. He'll help us. Please be OK. Please, please, please. I've nobody else to share my pasta with Mickey boy. Be strong my love. It will all be OK, I know it will." Her hands ran the length of his back, his eyes wide in panic, locked with hers. She wanted to phone Ben again, but he was on the way, it seemed like hours since she had found Mick. "Darling boy, you're OK, you just need some medicine, or something." Her hands held his head gently while they waited.

"Julia?" She heard Ben crashing through the long grass.

"Over here. Ben, we're here." He saw them and covered the distance fast. She stood up and got out of the way, watching Ben drop to his knees and examine the dog carefully. He sniffed near Mick's mouth, and felt along his stomach and chest.

"He's eaten poison. It's not unusual for farmers to put out stuff to kill rats. It's good he was sick, he probably got rid of some of it. I'm going to have to get him to the surgery, he needs a drip and I need to get as much out of him as I can. I'm going to carry him. Can you bring my bag?" She nodded, and watched Ben lift the dog into his arms, and followed with his bag. They struggled to the car, and loaded Mickey carefully. "Meet me at the surgery. OK?" She nodded and went back for the land rover.

The engine spluttered and coughed, then roared into life. She pulled forwards and out of the open gate into the road. Ben's car, with her dog in the back was gone, and she swiped her hand across her face, pushing her tears away.

The door of the surgery was open and pushing through, she could hear Ben talking softly to Mick. Reassuring, gentle, but not sugary. She followed the sound through to a room at the back of the building. Mick lay on his side on a table, his eyes were wide open and he was panting. She reached forward, her hand finding his silky coat. Ben already had the drip set up. His expression was grim, and she watched in silence, waiting for a glimmer of hope that the dog would be coming home with her.

"We see it quite a lot, sadly. Farmers put out poison to keep the rats down, but the rats are smart, they don't take it unless it's hidden in food. Then a dog comes along, and sees someone has left out something, scoffs the lot, and then we've got a fight on our hands. I won't lie to you, Julia, a fighting chance is all we have. I gave him something to make him sick when we got back here, so most of it is gone, we just have to counteract the part that has already been absorbed. The drip will do that, and I have given him something to help him relax, so he doesn't pull the needle out. OK. All we can do now is wait and see."

Her hand skimmed over the soft head, his eyelids fluttered but he was too sleepy to respond more than that. Her breath caught in her throat. Ben reached out and touched her arm.

"We're doing everything that can be done. He's young and strong, he has a really good chance."

"I should have checked. I should have known. I took him on without knowing what I was doing. I'm such a fool."

"No. You saved his life, he was a bag of bones, and you gave him a chance. Don't imagine you don't know what you're about. He's been lucky to find you." He guided her out of the treatment room and sat her down with a cup of tea and a biscuit.

14.

June 2018

Florian was getting used to the van he had bought, and he parked it close to the shop where he had watched the vet arrive with the dog, followed by Julia. He sat, watching the outside for any clue as to what was happening. The sun light reflected off the big window at the front of the shop and from where he was sitting, he couldn't see in. There was nothing he could do but wait.

An hour passed and then another. People passed him by, paying no attention to a man in a van, as they met friends or called into the pub. People were sitting outside in the warm evening air eating meals and looking happy and relaxed. Florian felt tense, his whole body on edge. The people enjoying their food and drinks could have been from a different planet for all they had in common with him. His jaw clenched, watching a family laugh and joke together. Next door to the pub was a small bakery. He had enjoyed the Cornish pasties he had tried, and decided he needed to eat something, so he slid out of the van and bought four, still warm from the oven. He unwrapped one, and bit into the soft delicious pastry. It would be the thing he would miss when he went home. His window was down and he rested his arm on the warm metal. Maybe one day, when he was more settled, he would be able to enjoy a simple meal like those people, perhaps he would have children who looked at him like those kids looked at their father, a woman who looked at him like that man's wife. He breathed deeply, holding himself in.

"He's breathing a bit easier. I'm hoping the drip is doing what it needs to." Ben smiled down at her. "It's going to be a long night, though. I'm going to close up the surgery if that's OK with you. You are welcome to stay with him, I will be here with him anyway. In case he needs anything." Ben stepped out through the door that separated the treatment room from the waiting area and lowered the shutters and locked the doors. He lifted Mick off the table and carried him through a side door, and up the stairs, to lay him on a soft fleece dog bed, next to the sofa, where he could hang the drip up on a hook on the back of the door. "Have a sit, I'll make some food. You must be hungry."

Julia sat. She watched the sleeping dog, her focus entirely on his softly rising and falling chest. Her mind turning circles through the day and back to when she last sat next to someone she loved, with a drip in their arm. Her Mum's face, soft and papery, the lines softened by sleep. Listening to the breathing, feeling the cool soft skin of her fingers. Willing her to get better. Coming as close as she ever had to praying. All her life, it had been the two of them, together, against the world. Sometimes they had struggled for money, and there had been times when the bills went unpaid, but Julia had never felt that she had missed out. She had been loved, of that she was certain. Whatever the truth was, about her mother, the love had been true.

Ben arrived back with plates of sausages and mashed potatoes.

"Sorry, this is my signature dish." He shrugged, passing her a plate.

"Looks great. I'm starving, so thank you. I'm no great chef either. It doesn't help that I don't really have a kitchen at the moment. I've pictured the kitchen I'd like and the furniture and everything. I've just realized, that all those pictures included Mick. Everything I had planned, I expected him to be a part of. He's so got to get better." She ate a mouthful of mashed potatoes, surprised to find they were soft and creamy. "Good potatoes."

"Thank you." He ate too.

"Will he be OK? I mean, if he makes it, will there be damage?" A tear slipped over her eye lid. She stroked his flank.

"There could be damage, perhaps liver, or kidney? It depends on what the poison was, but, let's not second guess this one. If he gets through tonight, let's worry about what comes next. OK?" He reached across to her hand.

"I know he's only been with me for a little while, but I can't imagine how I would be without him." She breathed out, a huff of frustration.

"I know, they are guaranteed to break your heart, no matter what." He wrapped his fingers around her hand, and she squeezed back.

The light was gone, and the pasty he had eaten sat heavily in his stomach. The seat in the van was uncomfortable, there was a bit of it that dug into his back. He wanted to get out and stretch his legs, but he sat still. The lights were on upstairs from the vet's surgery, and a knot of anger sat wrapped around the pasty. His sister was with the vet. The frustration he felt kept him awake and in his uncomfortable seat, watching the lit upstairs window, across the quiet street. Every bit of resentment he carried with him curled through his veins. Each time he had felt the weight of the guilt. It should have been him, his sister should have been safe, if only he had been at home. He was old enough to tell them who his Mum was. He would have been old enough to remember his home and his family. Nobody had told him that, but he had heard it running behind every word, every time they scolded him, and worse, the times his mother said nothing, just sat, holding the tiny blanket that had been left behind. His eyelids blinked down on gritty eyes, and he breathed deeply. His fingers loosened on the steering wheel, his mind let free, back to his childhood, and the constant reminders of the sister he had lost. Money had been beyond tight. There were often days when there was nothing to eat. There was no money for rent, so they lived with relatives, moving between his two aunts. His uncles felt no need to hide their feelings about their sister-in-law and her son eating the food they paid for. His mother grew more bitter and angry.

Florian had been glad to be able to go out and earn money, and give her an apartment of her own. He was even happier when he could afford to move out and live on his own, without her grey dark moods and her unpredictable bouts of anger. He visited every week, on a Tuesday, and gave her money to make the apartment comfortable, which sat in her cupboards, while the bare cold floors and the unpainted walls suited her moods. He tried, but his life had moved on, she stayed where she was, on her unforgiving furniture, with the heating turned off. His life was fun and the money he earned gave him freedom and choices. He noticed too late that she was thinner, and a little quieter.

Sitting with his thoughts for too long was pointless. He shrugged. She was clearly going to spend the night. There was no point in his waiting any longer. He stretched out his shoulders, and started the engine, and drove back to his bed, trying to ignore the pictures in his head of his sister and the vet.

Ben and Julia sat on the floor, with their backs against the sofa, her hand was still in his, and the dog slept on. His breathing was easier. His snores, more like his normal night-time sounds. As the fear and tension in her, slowly seeped away. Her eyes closed slowly, and her body gave in to the need for sleep. The warmth of him next to her soothed the muscles that ached and she drifted.

The daylight seeped through the slanted blinds and teased the edges of her eyes. Slowly easing herself back into the world, she opened her eyes to see the dog still sleeping. Ben was checking him.

"Is he OK?"

"He's much better. I've given him some more meds. He's working hard, fighting the poison. He needs time." He tilted his head to look into her face. "I'm telling you the truth, not sugar coating it."

"When will we know?" She spoke without taking her eyes from the dog's face.

"If he keeps on picking up, we'll see him start to come back by the end of today, or the start of tomorrow. I want to see him get to a point where he can drink, I'm putting fluids in through the drip, along with the meds, but hopefully, we can let it all wear off, and see what his reactions are like by this afternoon." He rested a hand on her shoulder. "How about some breakfast?"

"You've been so kind already. Yeah, breakfast would be great." She watched him walk away and then return with an empty milk container, waggling it at her while he leaned on the door frame.

"I won't be long. The little supermarket down the road will be open by now. The bread doesn't look too fresh either, so I'll get a loaf." He turned away from her.

"No, don't be daft, I'll go. Put the kettle on, and I'll be back." She pushed herself up from the floor and checked her pockets. She had some cash. He watched her down the stairs, and looked into the living room, where the dog snored. He heard the front door ping, and close, then crossed to the window to watch her walk away down the street, past his car, her land rover, and towards the shop. He half turned away, feeling a bit strange about watching her, when he saw the side door of a beaten-up old van slide open. She side-stepped but was off balance, and then recognized the man who stepped out onto the pavement next to her. He said something, and she shook her head, pulling away from him when he grabbed her hand. Then fighting with him as he bundled her into the van and slammed the door. Ben was running before he knew what he was going to do, following her route down the stairs and through the surgery. He reached the pavement to see the van pulling away into the road, her shouts of protest and her fists and feet loud enough to draw attention from people walking past.

Ben ran towards the van, desperately trying to remember the registration number, the make, the colour, anything that might help. His brain finally kicked in, and he pulled his phone out to take a picture.

The van roared down the street. He saw his nurse pulling up at the other end of the village, and shouted to her to look after the dog in his flat, and that he had eaten poison. She nodded, and he grabbed his keys from the surgery and started his car, following the van out into the country lanes, and hoping he wasn't already too far behind.

"Gemma. It's Ben. I need your help." He took a corner too fast, and prayed there was nobody coming the other way. "He snatched Julia, in a van, just grabbed her. I'm driving out of the village trying to find them, but I can't see anything yet. It's a faded blue citroen van, registration number BL03 HFF, I think, although the last letter could be an E, there's loads of mud on the plate. "

"Julia, with the dog?" She asked.

"Yes. The dog was poisoned yesterday, so I took him into the surgery. Oh shit. No, it's OK." He pulled the car back on track after avoiding a tractor. "She went out this morning to get some milk and he was waiting in the van. He grabbed her from the side door."

"Who was?"

"I think it's her brother, he certainly looked like her." He took a breath, pulling up at a cross roads. "I can't see him, and I don't know which way to go. What do I do?"

"Where are you?" He could hear a car door slamming.

"At the junction where you turn off to Welhouse Barn or Wooladon." He sat, looking at the roads, trying to force himself to think. He hit his head with the back of his hand. "Stupid. Of course, he's heading for the A30. He will want to get as far away as he can." His foot pushed hard on the accelerator and the car shot down the lane, headed towards the main road through Cornwall and away.

"Ben. Calm down. I've put it out for every car to be looking for them. CCTV are on it. I'm headed out too. Stay on the line and tell me where you are and if you see them stay back, OK?" Gemma was driving he could hear her car.

"Right, I'm driving down the lane towards the A30. He's been here a few weeks, so he'll know his way around, he'll know where he's going." Ben slammed on his brakes to avoid hitting a hatchback. "Come on!" He slammed his hand onto the steering wheel.

"What changed? Why take her today, not last week or yesterday?" Gemma could have been asking him or herself.

"I don't know." He nudged out around a tractor, but had to pull back in to avoid hitting a sports car. Slowly he pushed out again, putting his foot down when he saw the empty road. "I'm nearly at the A30."

"I've got people all over the place. They won't get far." Gemma shouted.

"I can see a blue van, please, please let it be them." Ben's voice shook. "Why would he take his sister, for god's sake. I've got three sisters, he could have any of them with pleasure. Get out of the way. Please." He dodged his way, changing lanes and going faster than he should. The blue van was in the fast lane, and he worked hard to get closer. He was two car lengths behind them. He was gaining on them but it was taking far too long.

"Can you see them, Ben?"

"I can see the van, I'm gaining on them. I need to get past this car and then I'll perhaps be able to see the registration plate." Ben checked his wing mirrors, and moved into the middle lane, put his foot down and passed the car, drawing level with the back of the van.

"Ben. Are you still there?"

"Yes. I'm, no, no, it's not them, it's not even the right blue. It's not even a citroen. I've lost them. Gemma help me!" He let his speed drop, the blue van leaving him behind.

"Take the next exit off the A30. I'll phone you back, once I've checked if anyone else has seen them." Gemma ended the call.

15.

The van smelled a bit stale. The floor and the sides were lined with wood sheets, and she landed heavily into one side as Florian pushed her in. Before she could get a breath back into her lungs, he slid the door back into place, with a bang, and next she heard the engine start.

Julia threw herself against the door, shouting as loud as she could, banging on the door, kicking the panels. Her eyes searched for the catch to open the side door, but it had been blanked off. The back door was the same. She beat the panels with her fists screaming until her lungs felt they would collapse.

The van took a corner that knocked her sideways.

"Florian! Florian! Why are you doing this? Please stop." She drummed her feet and fists against the side of the van. "Florian!" Her throat was raw with screaming. "Don't do this. Please. You said you were my brother, you should want to look after me, help me, not bloody kidnap me. Let me out, right now."

She rolled against the side of the van, as he took a corner. He was driving fast, perhaps someone had seen him take her, and they were being chased. The thought raised her hopes, and she pushed herself upright, her back resting against the door. The wood separating the driver's seat from the rear section of the van had no gaps so she could see no clues as to where they were going. She banged her fist on the partition.

She'd never felt so powerless or so angry. Her brain boiled with indignation, her skin prickled with the humiliation. He had overpowered her and overruled her choices. Had she allowed it? Should she had started fighting back more quickly? Had her politeness, her inhibition, been the reason he had been able to take advantage?

"Florian. Florian. Stop the van." A heavy beat drifted through from the cab, he must have turned on the radio to drown her out. She dropped her head into her hands and slumped against the side of the van. She could do nothing but wait, until he stopped the van.

Her head flopped forward, shocking her, she must have fallen asleep. How could she, in this situation? The van had stopped, perhaps that was what had woken her. She edged towards the side door, and listened hard. There was no sound. Slowly and very quietly she moved to the back doors, there was nothing. There was no sound from anywhere. She had to sit, and wait. It was frustrating to not know why Florian had done this, but it made her mad as hell that he had. If this was his plan, why not just grab her straight away, she lived in a shed for goodness' sake, in the middle of a field.

None of it made any sense. Her head ached from thinking about it. She needed some water, and something to eat. Trying to distract herself, she concentrated on listening again. The only thing she could hear was her stomach complaining. She closed her eyes, and saw her dog, lying as she had left him, with a drip attached to his leg. The guilt that rushed over her was shocking. He had only been in her life a few weeks, and yet she felt so completely responsible for him. She missed the soft fur and the way he nuzzled into her hand, and the warm weight of him when he leaned against her. He had already lost his first home, if she was in big trouble here, if Florian turned out to be some kind of murdering psychopath, then he would lose another. She should never have taken him on, who was she to take on an innocent dog, and let him believe she could provide a stable home for him? Her eyes were hot with tears. This was no good.

She needed to get out of this, and feeling sorry for herself, no matter how appealing, was not going to cut it. She sniffed, and wiped her fingers under her eyes. Shifting herself slowly across the van, she peered at the door. There was no visible mechanism to open the door. The wood covered the whole door, there were no gaps. It was gloomy inside the van, though, the only light came in through the small gap where the wood didn't quite cover the windows in the back doors. She edged towards the back of the van, where the light was slightly better.

The gap was tiny, and her fingers seemed huge as she tried to reach around the edges. It made no difference. There was nothing she could do.

The door to the cab opened.

"Julia?" It was a whisper.

"Florian? Please let me out." She tried to keep the wobble out of her voice, but it was there.

"I have to talk to you first. Please." A section of the wood moved to the side, and he pushed a bag through. It smelled delicious, and she pulled it towards her. It was warm, and she opened the bag. The pasty was fresh from the shop, and she took a bite.

"Thank you. I was hungry."

"It's OK." He turned in the driver's seat and watched her. "I want to talk to you. I know I shouldn't have taken you away, but I had some news, and I had to change my plans. I have to leave today. I want you to come with me." His face was sideways on to her, and looking at him through the small gap reminded her of films she had seen of people going to confession. She took another mouthful.

"So, let me out, and we can talk. I won't promise to come with you, but we can talk about it." She chewed, and bit again.

"I'll go and fetch some drinks, you will be thirsty when you finish that." He pushed open the door and climbed out.

She finished the pasty. It had tasted so good. They must, she supposed, still be in Cornwall then. She wiped her fingers on the bag. Her back was stiff with sitting on the floor of the van. She had no passport with her, so he would have to take her back home if he wanted her to go with him. Ben would have told people she was missing, they would be watching her shed, and her land. It would be OK. Whatever he thought he could make her do, she would be OK. The front door opened, and he slid a bottle of water to her. The plastic felt cold under her fingers.

"Where are you taking me, Florian?" She lifted her eyes to mee his. "Where?"

"I want you to help our mother. I would have asked you. I wanted to get to know you first, but things have changed, I ran out of time." His voice shrank to a croak.

"Where is she?" Julia shifted her weight so that she could see him more clearly.

"I will tell you all about it, as we drive." He turned away, to face the windscreen.

"I don't have a passport." She leaned back.

"You won't need one. Rest now. We have a long journey." He pulled away, and she sat back.

He was taking her somewhere in the UK then, where she needed no passport. That was a relief.

"Florian, what is your Mum like?" She rested her face against the wooden partition that separated them.

"She looked like you, when she was younger. She was bigger, you know, heavier. Her face though, you are like her. She is shorter. She was happy, she used to play with me, and sing to me, when I was little. Little by little she got, well, sadder I suppose. Angry." He took a deep enough breath for her to hear it. "She blamed my father for how her life turned out."

"Had they been happy, do you think? Before he came to

England?" She closed her eyes, trying to imagine what life would have been like if she had grown up in Albania. She had no point of reference or information to hang the idea on.

"I don't remember him really. I was very young. I remember you being born though. My Aunt came to stay, I went to sleep one night, and the next morning, you were there, wrapped in a blanket. She was so happy, crying and laughing all at the same time." He laughed to himself. "She couldn't tell him that he was a father again, we had no way of contacting him. She said it would be a good surprise when he came home." She could see his eyes watching her in the mirror. "You were a pretty baby, everyone said so. She used to hold me and you together in her arms and tell me how lucky we were, that our Papa was working hard to give us a good life. I suppose it was hard for her on her own. People talked." He took a deep breath. "My Aunt came and took me out to visit the shops, you were sleeping when we left, and my Mama said she would have a sleep too. When we got back the house was wrecked, and she had a bruise on her face, and cuts on her hands, and you were gone. She was sitting on the floor, with a little bear, a toy you had liked. She was so quiet. She cried, and hung on to the toy, but there was no noise around her. Police came, but they looked around and left, I don't think they even tried to look for you. She was different after that, broken." His voice shook a little. "I don't know why they took you. We heard from someone in the town that my father had stolen from his boss. It really didn't make sense to take a baby though, how could you pay what he stole. My Mama thought that you were taken as a punishment, to her, to him? Who knows?" He drove on in silence.

She rested her head back and wiped her tears away. She had been taken from a loving mother, for a debt. Could that be right? She had grown up with another mother, who loved her, gave her a good life, but the story she had heard was heart-breaking. The pain her Mother had been put through, the separation, it caught her anger, and extinguished it, like a bucket of cold water.

The road rumbled under the wheels of the van, and Florian seemed less interested in talking than he had been. She thought about the parents she had never met.

16.

May 2018

He had searched the old farmhouse and he thought he had found everything he needed. He was pleased to see that there were no neighbours to watch or wonder. Florian piled the paperwork he was going to take with him. Folders and envelopes mostly, and a locked box. He loaded them into his car and drove away. Five minutes of driving took him far enough away to feel safe to pull over and check what he had.

In the envelope, marked 'Janice's House', there was a copy of deeds, in the name of a property management company, to a house in London. Perfect. That must be where Janice lived. He could drive there as soon as he was ready.

Florian tapped the envelope with his name on the front. He would look at that later. The locked metal cash box was easy to unlock, his little screwdriver opened the lock smoothly. Inside, was, predictably, a pile of cash, and less expected, three different passports, one, Albanian, in his real name, one Polish, and one French, in different names. He shrugged and put them to one side. Underneath, wrapped in a cloth, and then in a piece of tissue paper, was a necklace, a gold chain, with the name Julia spelled out in diamonds. Who was Julia? He shrugged. She must have been important to the old man. The necklace must have cost a lot.

Slowly, he picked up the envelope. His fingers fumbled with the flap. After all the years, thinking his father was dead, then that tiny piece of information dropped by the father of one his friends. Research, months of checking, looking, searching for details about the man in England, who he thought at the time, had killed his father. The first picture of the man who looked back with features which were familiar, but at the same time, unknown. The rage, he could share with nobody else, the damage he felt in containing his feelings, not letting his mother see how angry he was. The more he discovered about his father, and the huge wealth he held, when they had lived a life filled with poverty and dependence, the angrier he became. Each step fuelled the fire that burned inside him. When he made the journey to Cornwall, and watched his father, saw that he lived alone, that he was old, and hunched over, and that he dressed in shabby old clothes, Florian was disgusted. He had expected an adversary, he came to find a man already broken by time.

He had wanted to shout and scream at the man, tell him all about what he had caused. There had been no time. The anger still simmered inside him. He had not had the chance to extinguish it.

Now he had to deliver his package, and then he could start the search properly. It meant a long drive, but that was no hardship. He turned on the radio and pulled away from the side of the road. Once he had arranged things, he had a night's sleep, and set out, back on the trail of his sister.

He decided to go to look for Janice, he knew from the research that he had done that she had taken his sister, so she was the one to follow. He had the address now, so he set his phone to direct him, and drove towards the motorway, and London. He drove through the gathering dusk and arrived outside the address in the early hours, which worked well for his purposes. The house was in darkness, but so were most of the houses in the street. The front gate and low wall led to a tidy garden. He slipped to the side of the house and found that by reaching over the top he could unbolt the gate and slip through into the back garden. He was angry that he had to have a childhood filled with risk and fear, but he had learned some useful skills along the way, and one of them was burglary. He smiled when he saw the sliding patio doors, his favourite. It took less than a minute, and he was inside the house.

The furniture was all in the property, but there was an empty feel to it. He walked through the rooms silently in the dark, and up the stairs. Nobody was there. The photographs on the walls were old and faded, but showed a pretty woman, playing with a little child, at various ages. One of the two of them together on the doorstep of this house.

The kitchen was empty, nothing in the fridge or cupboards. The cupboards upstairs were the same, empty. He prowled the house, looking for something, anything. The sun started to filter through the windows, and he was still searching. In the living room there was a small table which had a drawer on the side. Inside, he found a small piece of paper. He unfolded it, and sat heavily on the sofa. It was a death certificate. Janice was dead. She had been for years. This was a dead end, no clue to take him to his sister. He closed his eyes, resting his head down into his hands, and felt the weight of the failure on his shoulders. He sat still, knowing that he had nowhere else to go for a while, as the neighbourhood came to life around him.

Slowly he sat back up, facing the photos on the wall. Something struck him, none of them had been taken inside. No birthday cakes, no sitting on the sofa. None of them were posed either. Both of them looked as though they weren't aware the picture was being taken. These weren't family pictures; these were surveillance shots.

So, the old man had paid someone to follow them, take pictures. He had owned her house, or bought it after she died. Florian knew that his father had worked in London, so he had been reasonably close by. When did he move to Cornwall? Maybe, why did he move to Cornwall?

Florian's brain felt as though it was working double time, he felt breathless and a little nauseous. Yes. The date of the death certificate. It was six months before he knew his father had bought the little farm where he had found him.

So, she had died, and he had moved to the farthest reaches of the country. Not just to get away from London. Had it taken that long to settle his business? No, he could have moved faster than that. Had his sister moved there, and he had followed her? That could be true. He slipped the death certificate back into the drawer, and let himself out of the house. He needed to eat, and to search for his sister.

Thankfully records are everywhere, and Florian had learned how to search. He had found her on Facebook, smiling, and raising a glass of wine with friends, and adverts for the holiday business she owned, and in registrations on the Council websites for her business. She looked so like his mother, their mother, that he wanted to cry. She had been a few miles away from him when he visited their father. He had followed her there, to be close to her, when he had walked away from Florian and left him to fend for himself, to protect his mother, and to provide for them both. Now he knew who Julia was. The necklace made of diamonds was for his sister.

He chewed the sandwich parked outside the shop where he had bought it. He drank the juice and ate a small pie, which was too sweet, and hurt his teeth. He thought about what he should do next. He had to be clear, and not be angry like he had in the past. He needed to learn from that, and do better with his sister. He needed her, and she had to trust him.

He searched for a place to stay, and booked a room near to where she lived. He had time, he would get to know her and she could get to know him a little, learn to be family together. It would be the first time he had been family with anyone. His Mother didn't count. She had never counted. She had been too weak, too easy for his father to dismiss.

Before he started the drive back to Cornwall, he decided to open the envelope with his name on, that he had taken from his father's house. The flap slipped open under his fingers. He pulled a thick sheaf of papers out and lay them on the passenger seat beside him. On the top was a letter addressed to him.

Dear Florian

You found me. I thought you might. First of all, I am sorry, I walked away from your mother, we were unhappy together, and she wouldn't have accepted a divorce. I told myself that I did it to keep you both safe, my business was dangerous, and people could have hurt you to get to me, but it wasn't true. I did it to give myself the life I wanted, it was selfish, and I was a fool.

I know growing up in Albania with no money is hard, so, I have set up a business for you, I bought houses, which are rented out, they pay the rent in every month, the papers in this pack are all the deeds and the bank statements. It's all in your name, my son, and the money in the bank is yours.

Your sister is alive and well, she had no idea about me, or the life I lived. She grew up clean. There were times I wanted to help her, but I would have had to tell her things she didn't need to know. I have no right to ask you, but I will, please stay away from her.

I hope you have made a life for yourself, I think if you have found me then you have grown up smart. It's easy to say, don't make the same mistakes I did. I mean it, but I know that you are young, and have no reason to listen to me. I was angry, and stupid, and I hope that you are calmer and smarter than I was.

Have a good life, my son. Be happy, and strong.

Your Papa.

Florian's eyes burned with unshed tears. He was worried that his precious clean daughter would be dirtied by his discarded and abandoned son. He put the letter to one side. The deeds were all in his name, and the bank statement. He was a rich man. There were cards and the PIN numbers to take cash out of the bank. He took a breath. If his father had reached out to him, told him about this, before, would he have been so angry? He shrugged. It made no difference now. Carefully he tucked the papers back into the envelope, and sat back to close his eyes for an hour, before he drove to find his sister.

17.

June 2018

"How far are we going?" Julia called through to him.

"Not too far, just I want you to meet her. She's been waiting for so many years, she's been missing you for such a long time." He smiled.

"Kidnapping me was a bit over the top, why didn't you just ask me?" She had to raise her voice to be heard over the road noise.

"Would you have come with me?" He smiled to soften the words, and his eyes met hers in the mirror.

"No. Probably not. But, it would have been nice to have a choice. My dog's ill, he's eaten something poisoned. I don't want him to wake up, and find me missing." A tear slipped down her face.

"You'll be back soon enough. I couldn't risk you saying no. I'm sorry, but our Mama is not well, and I got a call, saying she was getting worse. She needs to see you before time runs out." He checked in the wing mirror, and changed lanes, pulling out past a lorry.

"What's the matter with her?" Julia shuffled forwards to be next to the gap in the partition.

"She's been ill a long time, she needs treatment, but the doctors need her to be strong enough to cope with it." He watched her in the mirror. "What was it like when you were a child? Where did you live?"

"I grew up in London, we moved around a fair bit when I was little, there wasn't a lot of money, so they were small places.

Then, when I was nearly eleven, my Mum got a better job, and she was approved for a mortgage, and bought a house. It was a small house, but we loved it there, we had a garden, and a bit more space. I got a bike, she taught me to ride it out in the garden." She thought back to those first bike rides. "I fell off a fair bit, and wobbled, but I got it in the end." She tried to think how she could get out. He was worrying her, she felt uncomfortable with him, and she was a prisoner here, there was no getting away from that. She knew he was her brother, there was no doubt of that, and she wanted to know about why she had been taken away as a baby, but he had shown another side of himself that put her nerves on edge.

"I used to ride everywhere around our town on my bike. It was very old, and the chain used to come off all the time, but it got me to where I needed to be." He watched her face carefully as he spoke. "What did you like the best when you were a kid?"

"I don't know how old I was, younger than eight, I suppose, and we used to make a play tent, putting sheets over the chairs, and cushions on the floor. I would take a sandwich and a drink in there, and pretend I was exploring in the jungle or something. I loved that. My Mum, er, Janice, used to encourage me to imagine and play like that." She closed her eyes, remembering the safe warmth of her little den, the soft cushions, and the drowsy feeling of the sunshine coming in through the sheets. For a moment she could smell the familiar scent of her mother's house, the washing powder, and something completely her Mum.

"She sounds like a nice lady. Mama was like that too, but she was so badly hurt when they took you. It was like she had something missing. A part of her, I mean, not you." He shook his head, frustrated.

"It must have been very frightening for her. Did you ever find out what happened to our father?" She saw his eyes check left and right. They were still on the motorway, he didn't need to.

"I always thought he died, when I was a kid, I found out he was living still after I came to England. He was a very bad man. Don't waste your time worrying about him." His voice was hard, and angry.

"Oh. Can we stop soon? I could do with going to the loo." She leaned back against the wood.

"Not for a while yet. We need to get a bit further on. You can wait, right?" What choice did she have?

She nodded and sat back. He wasn't ready to let her out of his sight yet, he knew as well as she did that she would be gone as soon as he did. Something about him made her frightened.

"Are you married, Florian?" She might as well find out as much as she could.

"No. I am not the type." He smiled, with no warmth in his eyes. "I like women, but I have never met one who made me want to give up all the others."

"I nearly was once. He was an idiot." She laughed. "He moved to Cornwall with me, we bought the business together, and it all went well. Until he decided it wasn't going fast enough for him, he told me we needed to take out a loan to upgrade the holiday lets. I thought it was too much money all at once, but I gave in. Stupid of me. The day after the money arrived in our account, he was gone, and the account was empty. It took me years to pay back the loan, and paint and refurbish the holiday lets with no money, but I did it. I learned a lot from the experience, but it was a tough time in my life." She closed her eyes, remembering the nights spent sanding and painting, and the disasters while she learned to make curtains and soft furnishings.

"Did you hate him?" There was an edge to his voice.

"No. Maybe. I was really angry. I was very hurt. Then I got on with it. I think I didn't have time to think about it too much. He moved away, and I removed his name from the business and the bank accounts. I think in some ways the work helped. I got past it. I don't hate him now. If I saw him, I'm not sure that we would have much to say to each other." She chewed the inside of her cheek. What she had said was true, there had been a time when she would have had loads to say to him, but that time had gone, and the anger with it.

"You would forgive him?" There was incredulity in his question.

"No, not forgive, but being angry at that level is exhausting, and pointless. It only hurts you, not the person you're angry with. Truly, I've moved on. I suppose he has too."

"You don't know where he is?" He was surprised.

"No, I expect he went back to London, but no, I don't know for sure." She shrugged. "I never heard from him again."

"I would have to find him, mess him up, if someone did that to me." His face in the mirror was hard.

"Everyone's different I guess." She felt the tension in her shoulders. There was something in the conversation that made her feel nervous.

"You never heard from him again?" He sounded so surprised.

"No." She had never thought about it before, but she had heard nothing at all, not from him or from friends. They had known loads of people together in London, who she was still in touch with, but none of them had mentioned hearing from him either. Perhaps they were just being polite, not telling her. She shrugged, it really meant nothing now. "Tell me some more about your life."

"I moved here when I was fifteen. I got into some trouble at home, and my Uncles wouldn't have me in their houses anymore. I went to live in Scotland, because somebody told me that it looked like Albania." He laughed. "It didn't, but I liked it there. We spent some time in Dundee, then a few years in Edinburgh. Have you been there? Some of it is very beautiful.

Mostly cities look the same, wherever you are."

"I went once, years ago now, with my Mum. I think we went into the mountains a lot." She shrugged.

"I will take you, one day. I can show you the good bits. I like the people there, they are more honest. I moved to London, but I found people there were almost unable to tell the truth, I ended up in Manchester." He shook his head.

"What happened, when you got into trouble?" She shifted her weight to try to find somewhere more comfortable.

"I got into a fight. Nothing terrible, just normal teenage stuff." He squinted against the sunlight.

"So, you and your Mum decided to come here and start a new life?" She smiled, thinking she was being encouraging.

"Our Mum. She's your Mum too."

"Sorry Florian, it's a lot to take in."

"I know. No, we didn't come together. I came first, on my own." He took a breath. "I got on a plane, and I landed in Scotland. When I made enough money, I sent a ticket for my Mum."

"How did you do that when you were fifteen? What about school?" She was genuinely shocked. "When I was that age, I couldn't have looked after myself. I was hopeless."

"I looked older. I got work, on a building site, I carried stuff up and down ladders, I dug holes and mixed concrete. I earned next to nothing but it fed me and paid for a room to sleep in. I even saved up so I could send money home. I wanted to prove them wrong." There was more than a little pride in his voice.

"How long did you do that for?" She edged a little closer to him.

"Nearly six months. I knew the boss was taking advantage of me, he knew I was underage but I was cheap labour. Then I hit sixteen and I moved on, made better money, and showed my Uncles how wrong they had been." There was bitterness in him, real and very hard. "We'll stop here, and I'll get some food. There's no bathroom here for you, but I can find a bowl for you to use, OK?" He pulled into a parking space and opened the door before she could argue.

18.

June 2018

"Gemma. Any news?" Ben was parked, he had no clue where to go next to look for her. His hands were spread on the steering wheel, stretched wide.

"Ben. Go home. I've got every police car in the County looking for them. I've also told Devon and Dorset. They won't be able to hide for long. If she gets away from him, she will come back to find her dog. Come on. Let us do this." She was calm, and that helped to bring him back to where he could think.

"Will you ring me, as soon as you know anything?" He closed his eyes, his breathing slowing.

"I promise I will."

"OK. Anything at all?" He wanted to be sure.

"Yes. Go home Ben." The line went dead.

He drove slowly, checking the gaps between hedges, taking lefts and rights, had he gone off the main route, not straight to the main road. There was no blue van to be seen anywhere. He pulled onto farm yards, and asked if they had spotted anyone. There was nothing.

He pulled up in front of his surgery, ran his hand over his face, and tried to pull it together. He shouldered open the car door and went in.

"Ben? What happened?" His nurse jumped up, and pulled him through to the treatment room. "Tell me."

"He grabbed her off the street. I watched him pick her up and throw her in a van. I ran, but I wasn't fast enough. I chased them in the car, but I couldn't find them." He buried his head in his hands.

"Come and sit down, come on. We'll wait to hear from the Police together. They've got more chance of finding her than you have. They have more experience. Who is he, why would he take her?" Her head tilted to the side.

"He's her brother. She didn't even know she had a brother a couple of weeks ago. He turned up with a story about her being abducted as a baby. Now he's taken her." His eyes opened wide. "Do you think he poisoned the dog?" He stood up and paced the small room. "How did he know she would be here?" He pulled open the door through to the hallway, and pounded up the stairs. He ran his hand over the soft fur on the dog's head. Nothing had changed, he checked the dog's gums and lifted his eyelids. He was stable.

He sank down onto the sofa, stunned by how angry he was. A week ago, he was trying to get himself together enough to even ask this girl out, now he was in bits, and chasing speeding vans around the countryside. The floorboards outside the door creaked. Jess, his nurse, poked her head around the door. She held a cup of coffee in front of her.

"I've asked Carrie to come in and cover your surgery." She held out her hand to stop his arguments. "You are in no fit state. It's my decision as practice manager. You're no use to the animals down there as you are." She handed him his coffee, and he took it, gratefully.

"I didn't realize, how much she meant to me. I must be a complete idiot. I just stood at the window and watched him take her." His eyes blinked and he pushed himself to focus. His phone rang, and he jumped up to pull it from his pocket. "Hello?"

"Hi Ben. It's Gemma. I promised to let you know, so I am. We've found the plates, from the van, he's changed them. It suggests to me that he has planned this, and that he is still in the van. We have widened the search area, and to all blue vans. I have asked Devon, Dorset, Somerset and Wiltshire to be watching for them too. I'll let you know as soon as anything else happens." She took a breath. "We'll keep looking until we find her Ben."

"Thanks Gemma." He said, but she was already gone. He slumped back onto the sofa. Jess hovered in the doorway.

"Carrie just sent me a text. I'm going down to help her run the surgery. Don't go anywhere. I'll be back in a bit. OK?" She waited for his nod, then he heard her steps on the stairs. Just like he had listened to Julia's steps. He checked his watch, had it really been only an hour and a half ago? It seemed like days. The dog snored, and called him back from his thoughts.

He sat on the floor, where Julia had sat, next to the warm sleeping dog. He closed his eyes and remembered the weight of her warm body leaning against his. He wanted, more than he could imagine wanting anything else, to go back to that, to then, and have her stay.

Why though? Why to so many questions, why did he take her at all, and why from here? She lived in a garden shed. He could have taken her from there, and nobody would have known for ages. What could he gain from this?

Had the fact that he had started seeing her made her brother angry? Could that be what had tipped him over the edge, made him decide to grab her?

One thing was for sure, going around in circles wasn't teaching him anything new. If anything at all, it was just making him more stressed and less able to think. He knelt by the dog, checking his breathing was steady, and that the drip was running smoothly. He stroked the soft nose. If the only thing he could do for her now was to look after her pet, then he would do the best he could. He focused his energy entirely on caring for the animal and found it helped him as much as Mick.

19.

She took the sandwich he offered, and put it on the floor of the van. The bottle of water he passed through the gap reminded her painfully of her need to pee.

"Florian. Please. I can't pee in a bowl. Please let me use the toilet. Come with me if you don't trust me. I just need to go. Please." She held her stomach, crunching over.

He sat in the cab, thinking about it. He was watching her in the mirror. "Tell me why I should."

"Because you're my brother. You don't want me to be uncomfortable. I am coming with you to meet our mother. I don't want to turn up smelling of wee." She gave him a hopeful smile. "Also. Wouldn't you rather I went with you to meet her willingly, rather than being unhelpful and you dragging me there?"

He shook his head. "OK. But please, don't make me come and get you. I don't want to have to, but I will." He locked eyes with her, and she believed him. His eyes were hard, his glare fixed, there was no anger there, just a promise that he meant what he said.

"I won't let you down." She was surprised to find that she meant it. Her intention, all the way through this, had been to get away at the first opportunity, but something was changing in her head. She wanted to go home, to see her dog, and Ben, to see her friends again, and build her home, get back to normal. There was another part of her though, which was curious. She wanted to meet this woman who had loved her from a distance, and had been so sad from missing her. In some way, she was curious to see this woman. She had no memory of her, but she wanted to know who she was, before it was too late.

The side door slid open and Florian reached in for her hand. They walked towards the small service station and he guided her through the front doors. Inside the ladies, there was only one toilet, one mirror, one sink. She quickly went to the loo, and was grateful. What she wanted was a way to let people know she was OK. There was nothing, absolutely nothing in the little room. She ran the tap and washed her hands. Her knee knocked against the panel under the sink, and it moved. Slowly she crouched down in the tiny space. The panel was loose, it slid under pressure from her fingers. In the space behind it, were cleaning materials, she pushed them to one side, and checked the back of the cupboard. Nothing. She ran her fingers around the sides of the cupboard and along the edges. There was nothing there. She slumped back and stood up to rinse her hands again. She dried them on the roller towel. Opening the door, she found Florian waiting. He pulled the door open, and stuck his head inside. Satisfied that she had not left a message anywhere he held her hand and they walked back to the van.

"You did what you said. I wasn't sure you would." He smiled at her as he opened the back door.

"Where are we going Florian?" She stood still, waiting for an answer.

"To see our mother." He guided her in to the back of the van. "Eat your sandwich." He drove away, and back onto the motorway. "You think you do not know me, but I don't know you either. I have to learn to trust you, the same as you need to."

"So, talk to me, tell me about yourself, so we can get to know each other." She opened her sandwich. "What was it like when you came here? Did you already speak English?"

"I spoke a little, just enough to get by, but I learned every day. I watched TV and I went to shops, learned to chat a bit more each day. I got things wrong, but slowly I got the words I needed. The better I got, the more confident I was, and I earned more money. By the time I got enough together to send money home, I was almost speaking like I do now. I worked with people from this country and from my home. But we all spoke most of the time in English." He took a breath. "I didn't know back then that our father was still alive. If I had, I would have gone to see him then, before I brought our mother here, but I found out later. I suspected, only because of something somebody said, not because they knew something, but it gave me a clue."

"What did they say?" She sat close to the gap between the front and back of the van.

"He said that criminals from our country were making good money in London, and he had heard that they all changed their names so that if they were arrested, the police weren't able to trace them back to their homes, and so that their families were safe from other criminals." He shrugged his shoulders. "It made me wonder about whether our father might have changed his name, and made up the story that he had died. It was only recently, that I met someone who knew him, who recognized me, because I looked like him. He assumed that I knew that he was alive, and I played along, so that he would tell me more. Once I had the name he had used, I started to look properly. I found all sorts of information. Eventually I found him." His eyes met hers in the mirror.

"You found him? Our Father?" She sat up straight.

"Yes. I found him, before I found you." His eyes flicked to the side to check the traffic.

"Did you like him?" She asked. "I mean, I know you were angry with him, but did you like him?"

"I don't know if I liked him or not. I didn't get the chance to get to talk to him much." His face was still.

"Does he live in England?" It was hard for her to understand why she was having to ask him so many questions, why he was so reticent. Perhaps he had been upset not to be able to get to know his father. Perhaps he was still angry with him.

"He lives in Cornwall. I think he followed you down there. I think he wanted to be near you. I don't know for sure." He caught her eye in the mirror and smiled.

"Really? He lived near me? I could have walked past him in the street and not known it was him." She was shocked to find that she wanted to cry. "I wish he had got in touch, talked to me."

"He asked me to give you some things. I have them for you. He wanted you to have them." He watched her closely.

"What sort of things?" In her mind, she remembered going through her Mum's things when she died. The bits she had kept, the pictures and the birthday cards she had no idea her Mum had kept for years, sparkly bits of card, with crayon squiggles. They had meant something to her Mum and she had been so touched to know that they had been saved.

He passed an envelope through the gap. It said Julia on the front. She looked carefully at the writing, it looked familiar, but not. It was a little bit similar to hers, but different, spikier, somehow. She turned the envelope over, and opened the flap. It was a large envelope, and she reached inside. There was a cold piece of metal, and her fingers wrapped around it. She pulled it out, jingling against itself as it came out of the envelope. It was gold, and heavy. The chains on each side were thick. The mid-section spelled out her name in stones. They looked like diamonds. It was definitely not something she would have chosen for herself. It was clunky and thick, but the fact that someone had chosen this for her, wanted to give her something which must have cost a fortune and told her that they had cared about her, and knew her name. Why hadn't he come and talked to her then? What would she have said if someone had turned up and said they were her father? She laid the necklace on her lap, and pulled out the rest of the things in the envelope. There was a photo, an old one, creased white in one corner. A man, who looked a lot like Florian, holding a tiny baby. Was that her? In the photo he was in a room that looked like an office. She peered closer at his face. She wanted, so much, for it to tell her something. She laid the photo down, and looked through the rest of the papers. There were some deeds to a house, in her name. Her eyes sprang open, it was her Mum's house. He must have bought it from the property management company she sold it to. Her eyes filled with tears. It had been so hard to sell the house where she grew up, harder than anything she had ever had to do. Clearing her Mum's stuff out, had broken her heart, but saying goodbye, permanently, to that house had been beyond difficult. Whoever her father was, he had understood that. She ran her hand over the deeds, then wiped a finger under her eye. There was also a small envelope, which held some more photos, of her Mum, and her Father, of her Mum on her own, all dressed up, looking so glamorous. Finally, one of her Mum, holding her, she knew it was her, from the look on her Mum's face. She knew that look. She knew that baby was her.

"Florian, these are amazing. The photos. Aren't there any more recent ones of our Dad?" She shuffled forwards.

"There might be. I suppose there will be stuff at his house." He shrugged. "Do you like the necklace?"

"It's not my kind of thing, but I like that someone wanted to choose me something. I wish he'd come to see me, instead of buying jewellery." She chewed her bottom lip gently. "Perhaps I met him and I didn't know. Or saw him somewhere, without knowing it was him."

"Maybe. He didn't live far from you. It's possible." He looked carefully at her in the mirror. "You're upset? Crying?"

"No, well, maybe a little bit. He left me my Mum's house, I had to sell it, and it was so hard. I felt like I was walking away from my Mum and my childhood and everything that I loved and cared about. He must have understood how I felt about it, to buy the house back for me." Her voice cracked and she wiped a tear. "I wish I met him when he was living near me. Where does he live now?"

"Well, never mind that at the moment, you get to meet your mother instead. We can be with her in a couple of hours. She will be so happy to see you. She doesn't know yet that you are coming. I didn't want to tell her until I knew for sure." He smiled to himself.

"Does she speak English? Will she be able to understand me?" She shifted her weight to try to find a comfortable place to sit.

"She speaks a little, not as clear or as good as mine. She understands though. I think you will like her. I know she will be overjoyed to see you again." He laughed. "I feel like I'm on one of those TV shows. You know, here is your long-lost daughter, we've brought her all the way from Australia."

The road ahead looked the same, it was motorway, mostly with light traffic. For some of the time, Julia held her new necklace in her hands and thought about the man who had bought it for her. She imagined what he would have looked like as an older man. White hair? Bald? How would his face change, would it be wrinkled, or saggy? She imagined walking through the supermarket, and passing him, not noticing an older man. Or had he spoken to her, made a choice to say 'good morning', or to touch her arm, hold open a door for her in a shop? It was the sort of thing that could drive somebody insane. Clearly Florian was holding back something about her father, but she would have to wait, until he was ready to tell her.

"So, what's wrong with your Mum? You said she was ill." Julia packed away the gifts from her father.

"She has a rare blood disease. It's a kind of cancer. They told me the name but it's really long. I have it written down. She has had loads of treatments, most of them seemed worse than the illness. She doesn't like to be in the hospital, she doesn't always know what to say to the nurses. But a new care worker started last week from Albania also, and they get on, so she is happier." He stayed looking straight ahead. No eye contact. It made Julia uncomfortable.

"Can they do other treatments?" Julia was going to meet her mother, and maybe only just in time to lose her again.

"The doctors said there might be another way forward, they will tell me when I get there. My Mum was a bit unsure about what they said." He shrugged. "Only another hour, perhaps."

She looked at the road through the gap. "Is she in London?"

"Yes. She is not far from the house where you grew up. Your house now, I suppose." He smiled at her.

"How did you find me? You never told me." She sat back against the side of the van and waited. He stayed quiet for a few moments, perhaps he was gathering his thoughts.

"When my Mum got sick, I spent a lot of time sitting in the hospital. There was nothing I could do, except think and read. I took my laptop in with me, and I started searching for my father. I thought he might be able to tell me where you were, and she might feel better if she could meet you. It took a long time, a lot of research, but I found him. He was able to tell me where Janice lived. I hoped to trace you through her. He didn't tell me where you were. I went to the house where Janice lived, but she was gone, and I found out that she had died. Then I realized that he moved to Cornwall soon after she had died. I thought maybe he had moved there because you lived there. You were the easiest one to find. Everything in your name, Council Tax, Electricity. I went to your old house, near to Constantine Bay, and they told me where you had gone." He paused. "I'm glad I found you." He smiled at her, and she believed him. She wanted to tell him that she was glad too, but although she was glad to have a brother, she was unsure if she would have chosen him. "OK. Your turn."

He told her in the mirror. "Tell me what your favourite memory of your childhood is."

"Um." The pictures flooded into her mind. "OK. There was this day, it was warm, summertime, and we played, all day, we put up a tent in the dining room, and left the back door open. We read stories together, and then Mum said we had to eat something, so she made a picnic. We sat in the tent, eating crisps and apples, and, I don't remember what we ate. When it was bedtime, we curled up right there, and tucked blankets around ourselves, we cuddled up and we slept until the morning. It's hard to explain, but it felt like there was just us two, in the whole world. She made me feel like that. She made me feel that the world was a safe place. It must have been hard for her, if our Dad was as bad as you say, but she never let me see that she was frightened, or anything." She wiped a tear. "This is the most I've cried in a long time."

He turned off the motorway and they drove through streets where there were houses. It seemed slow after the motorway. She recognized the roads. They drove through Rickmansworth and into Northwood. He pulled into the car park at Mount Vernon Hospital. He had to buy a ticket to park, and while he was gone, she tried to tidy up her hair, she wanted to look nice, didn't want to be a disappointment to her mother who had been waiting for this moment for such a long time. How horrible would it be if, after all the waiting, they disliked each other the first time they met?

Florian came back and put the ticket on the window. He opened the side door and let her out. The light was bright and surprising. She shielded her eyes with her hand.

"Come on." He led her into the building, past the reception area, and up the stairs. The corridors were quiet, and smelled of cleaning fluid. They had to pass through a security door, then into a room with four beds. In the corner, by the window, was a woman who looked like Julia, older, smaller, but there was no doubt, this was her mother. She stood still, strangely shy to meet the woman they had talked about. Florian was talking softly, not in English, his head close to his mother's. He beckoned to Julia, and held out his hand to her. She stepped forward, almost tripping on fresh air.

"Hello." The woman in the bed turned her head to see where the voice had come from. Her eyes blinked, and filled with tears. She wrapped her hands around Florian's hand, speaking fast, crying, catching her breath and starting again.

Julia stood, not sure what to do, if she rushed in, would that be rude? Should she wait until her mother calmed down a little? She stepped forward slowly, and reached out a hand to bridge the gap. No, there was no question. She had to touch the hand that reached out to her. She sank to a chair by the bed, and felt the strong fingers of her mother wrap around hers. Her other hand chased the shape of her daughter's face. Tears sprang from her eyes, and her mother, for the first time in many years, wiped them away.

"Anya." It was said carefully, with such strength of feeling. "Anya."

"Was that my name? When I was a baby?" She checked with Florian. He nodded.

"I'm so sorry, that you have been ill. Florian has told me all about you." Their hands were wrapped around each other. It sounded too formal and stilted to speak to her mother this way, but they were strangers, and neither spoke the other's language well enough to really talk.

"You grown up beautiful." Her Mother's face lit up with joy. Her eyes were so filled with happiness and light. "Thanks to you, Florian. For finding my girl."

The doctors came on their rounds, talking to the lady in the next bed first. The curtain they pulled around gave little privacy. Then they came to speak to Katya. The main doctor looked tired.

His sleeves were rolled up to above his elbows and his trousers fit him badly.

"Good afternoon. I am Doctor Harris, we've met before. You're the son, I remember you." He turned to Julia. "Hello, we haven't met."

"This is my daughter. Anya." She beamed at the doctor. "She has come to see me. To help me."

"Great, that is very good news. May I speak to you, Anya? Perhaps if you could come this way?" He nodded to them all and turned to walk away. Julia followed him slowly, and found that Florian was with her. Outside the ward, on the corridor, the doctor waited for them. "As your brother will have explained, your mother is in a very bad way. She needs a bone marrow transplant. Your blood test was a match, which is incredible luck. Unfortunately, your brother was not compatible. We need to get started as soon as we can. There are some forms to fill in, and then we can take a stem cell donation from you. It really is a very simple procedure, and then we can give your mother the treatment. I'll fetch the forms. Won't be long." He turned and walked away towards the main doors of the ward.

"What?" Julia felt a rushing sensation in her head. He had brought her here to take her bone marrow. "What the fuck, Florian?" She shook her head, trying to clear the noise and the shock. The wall behind her seemed the only solid thing in the whole building.

"Julia, please. I know I went about this wrong, but everything I told you was true. She has missed you all your life, and she'll die without this. I wanted to have time to talk to you, let you get used to being part of the family, but there isn't time. She'll die without this. I checked it out, it's not as big a deal as it sounds. Please Julia. Please save my Mum. Please be my sister. I didn't care about you, when I first found you. I just wanted to save my Mum, but I've got to know you, I want to be your brother, I want us both to have time with her. Please. I'm begging you."

97

His eyelids blinked over wet eyes. She was too angry and, if she was honest, too hurt by what had happened, and how he had behaved.

She turned towards the door of the ward, and through the window, saw her mother waving. Her birth mother, who had waited to meet her all her life, if that was true. This sad old lady who had lost time waiting for her daughter. Julia closed her eyes and thought of the mother who had brought her up, gentle, kind Janice, who had cuddled her through illness and taught her the right way. She wanted Janice to stand next to her now, help her with this.

20.

"Gemma? We've found something at the site, I think you should probably have a look. I've called in forensics." He took a breath. "It's a body, or at least part of one."

"Right. OK. I'm on my way." She hung up. "Keep me informed if they find anything on the missing woman. OK?" She grabbed her keys and drove to the farm. When she had last been there, it had been full of officers and the RSPCA. The owner, who she now suspected had been a person of interest to the Met was missing. She had talked to Serious Crimes on the phone, and sent over what she had, and their preliminary response had been positive. She parked on the lane and walked in. "Right, what have we got?"

"Over here." The young sergeant led the way. "Forensics say the body has been here a few years. They are saying male." She reached the area, and looked down to the shallow grave.

"Oh. Right. So, have you got a clue if its less than five years, more than?" The man in the white jump suit turned his head.

"Not yet. I've only been here ten minutes myself. I want to get the remains back, and run some tests. Were you expecting this?" She shook her head and he shrugged.

They backed away. "How did you find it?"

"You said to look through his papers. I went through everything. There was a pile of photos. I don't know who they are. There were papers about this place, when he bought it, I suppose. Then there was this." He handed her an evidence bag with several teeth inside, broken, and dirty, but definitely teeth.

"Why did this make you look for a body?" She raised her eyebrow at him.

"It didn't. I didn't realize what they were first of all, I picked them up, then, when I worked it out, I felt a bit, well, sick. I went out for some fresh air, and I walked over to the fence there, between the barn and the house. I thought, this is a stupid place to put a fence. There's no way a farmer would put a fence there. It stops you turning any animals out of the barn, straight into the field, you'd have to take them around the back of the barn, what a waste of energy. So, I walked over to the fence, and one of the posts was loose. I knew he had a cow, perhaps when he was younger, he had more than one. He had chickens too, but they were over the other side. This fence wouldn't keep chickens in. The patch of earth where the fence was, it was flat, not walked on. Like, it wasn't used. I thought, that's what the fence does, it stops people or animals walking on this bit of land. There was a shovel in the shed, so I dug up a couple of feet, and sure enough, there was the body." He looked pleased with himself.

"Well, I'm not sure that I follow your reasoning, but it got the result. I wouldn't have tied that together. Good work, thank you." She smiled. "This place is full of secrets. We still aren't completely sure who the owner is, and now there's a body. Its Jake, isn't it?" The sergeant nodded. "OK, Jake, come and show me what else you found."

"Like I said, there are photos, some were taken locally, others could be anywhere." He held out a neatly stacked pile of photographs.

She flicked through the first few. "I know this girl. Jesus, I spoke to her the other day." She carried on checking through them. "This is her, but younger. He's been watching her, maybe for years. She pushed the photos into an evidence bag. "Tag these." She passed them back to him. "Anything else?"

"The papers I told you about. Some bills, normal stuff, all paid. There was a letter from a hotel down the coast a little bit, apologizing that they couldn't find something he had left behind. Loads of junk mail. He liked the scratch cards. There were quite a few of those. There's a safe, or at least some kind of strong box, behind this book case. You can't see it until you pull the books out, perhaps he didn't use it, in any case, it's locked. There were a few bottles of brandy. Not cheap stuff either. A Christmas card from the vets and one from someone called Gerry. And of course, the books. There must be over a thousand of them. If it's OK with you, I'll go through them and make sure nothing's hidden between them or anything."

"Yes. Crack on with that. Let me know if you find anything. Well done. Make sure forensics take those teeth with them." She left him to it and walked outside. She looked at the fence, where the forensic officers were still busy. Now that he had pointed it out, it made sense. There was no reason to have a fence there. Farmers, he was right, were not quick to put up a fence unless it served a purpose. She took out her phone.

"Ben? Hi. I haven't any news on Julia, but I need to talk to you. It seems you were right, there is a connection between the farm, and her. Can you tell me, how long was he a client of yours? Mr Alex?"

"At least five years, perhaps a bit longer." He took a moment. "No, I'm wrong, it was longer, he was one of the first I took on, when I came back down here after Uni. So that would be closer to seven."

"OK. When you used to come up here, was there a fence between the barn and the house?"

"Between the barn and the house? Oh, no, he put that in because of Eric."

"Eric who?"

"Sorry, no Eric the bull. He used to get out sometimes from the farm down the road. One time he got into another farm, he was quite aggressive. I asked Mr Alex what the fence was for and he said he wanted to put off the bull if he got out again. Slow him down or something. I think he was nervous of bulls. Fair enough, Eric was a couple of tons of angry most of the time." He waited.

"OK. But the bull never actually got to his farm?"

"Not as far as I know."

"Thanks Ben, I'll keep in touch when I know anything." She hung up, and slid her phone into her jacket pocket.

"Boss? I found some keys and one of them opens the safe. I think you should look at this." Jake was standing in the doorway, and he ducked inside as she walked towards him.

She had to kneel down to get level with the safe. Inside there were stacks of twenty-pound notes, and two hand guns. "Shit." She shuffled backwards on her knees. "Get Forensics in here, before they take the body and get them to take the guns. I want to know when they were last fired. Between you and them, bag up this money. Keep looking." She stepped out of the room, then thinking better of it, back in. "Everything by the book please." He nodded. "Thank you."

She walked back out into the yard, and looked around. What had this man been up to?

"Gemma. We've found something." She walked over. "There's a wallet, in with the body. There's cash in it, and a bank card. I think a driving licence too. Says his name is Michael Spencer."

"Great. Can I look, or do you need it?" He passed her an evidence bag, and she could see the cards and the wallet through the plastic. Carefully, she took a picture with her phone, of the licence, and the bank card. "Thank you. Let me know when you find anything else?"

She climbed back into her car and made some notes on the

pictures. She put in a phone call to check on the licence, and whether he was registered as owning a car, and to find out how much this man was holding in his bank account, and when he was last heard from. It appeared he did own a car, which had been left parked in a car park in Tintagel, and eventually it had been towed away, nobody had claimed it. The bank said that he had over twenty-five thousand pounds in his account, which was still there, and had remained there for over five years. He had made no payments and there had been no activity on his account since then.

Gemma sat back and took a breath. It seemed likely that this was the man who was buried then. Whoever killed him didn't do it to get at his money. There was cash in his wallet still. He had really upset somebody. She watched while the body was loaded into the back of the mortuary van, and was about to leave when she saw them pull something else out of the hole.

"Boss? There's a bag in there too. They'll have a better look when they get back, but it looks like he was going on holiday or something, there's clothes and shaving stuff, and a phone. Maybe a long weekend? It's a nice bag too, leather, expensive looking."

She nodded. "OK I'll wait for the call. See if you can turn up anything else here, then make your way back. I want to know as much as we can about the guy who lived here. When you get back, start looking in to Michael Spencer and see what you can find out about him. His bank was in Padstow, so he was local, they had an address for him in Tintagel, so I'll drive up and have a look at that, seeing as you're doing so well with the digging." She smiled, and he nodded and walked back into the house. He was only a few years younger than her, and he was keen, and good at his job. She was lucky to have him.

Tintagel was a little too busy being a tourist attraction that morning, almost every shop was called Merlin's something or other, and there were signs directing everyone to the castle where the magic of Cornwall had been woven into every rock and blade of grass. The car park was easy to find, but it had been more than five years, and it was just a piece of land which charged extortionate prices to leave your car there, paid into a machine. The address the bank had given her was a house off the high street. Nobody answered at the door, so she wandered up the high street to the only estate agent to see if she could find out any more.

Her badge got her through the front line of heavily made up girls and a young man wearing too much aftershave, and into the manager's office in the back of the shop. The manager stood up and leaned across the desk to shake her hand, he was a short man and his stomach restricted how far he could reach.

"Craig Henton. How Can I help?" She would have picked him out as an estate agent in a crowd. Very dapper. A little too smug.

"I'm trying to find out about a property around the corner, and I wondered if you could tell me anything about it?" He nodded. "14 Atlantic Way."

"Ah, yes, 14, we rented that one about three, no closer to four months ago. We have been looking after the property for a few years now. The landlady lives in the village."

"I'm interested in someone who gave that property as an address, a little over five years ago. Would you have been involved at the time?" She waited while he called the file up on his computer.

"Do you have the person's name?" He nodded to himself. "Yes, we were renting the property then."

"Michael Spencer." She watched his face change from smooth to surprised.

"Ah yes, the mystery man. He signed the rental agreement, picked up the keys, and never moved in, we never heard from him again. We phoned, obviously, he had paid a deposit, and a month in advance, but when we couldn't reach him, and the property was still empty, and no payment came in for the second month we re-advertised." He sat back, his fingers interlaced over his stomach. "I always thought he must have patched it up with his wife or whatever and gone home."

"Did he tell you that was why he was moving here?" She sat a little closer to the desk.

"No, I just thought that. We wrote to his old address, to try to refund his deposit, but there was no response."

"You have a previous address?"

"Oh yes, of course. I'll print it off for you." He smiled and clicked the mouse. The printer behind him whirred into life. "Here you are. I hope it helps. Will you let us know, what happened to him? I've always been curious."

"You've been very helpful. Thank you. I'm sure it will all become public record at some point, Mr Henton." She took the paper from him and read the address.

She bought a pasty for lunch from Merlin's Kitchen, and joined the tourists walking back to her car, taking bites as she went. She had nearly finished when she got back to the car. She checked her ticket, she had five more minutes to go before it ran out, so she pulled out the address again, that would be her next stop.

The bay sparkled in the sunshine, as she drove through the gateway. The view was fantastic, postcard perfect. The little holiday let chalets were painted in soft creams and pastels. It was Cornwall with its best foot forward. She climbed out of her car and looked around, there was a reception area, which looked the same as all the other little buildings. A woman walked out, wearing a soft pink shirt and a pair of knee length white shorts.

"Hello? Mrs Shelton?" She was welcoming, friendly.

"No. I'm from the police." Gemma showed her warrant card. "I need to talk to the owners."

"That's me. Well, me and my husband. I'm Miranda Clancy, my husband is George. He's not here at the moment." She gestured with her hand towards the reception area. "Would you like to come in?"

Gemma followed her inside, and sat down with her. "I am looking for someone called Michael Spencer."

"Doesn't mean anything to me. Would he maybe be booked in to arrive shortly? I can have a look." She started to get up.

"No. he gave this as his home address a little over five years ago." Gemma watched carefully, there was no change in her expression at all.

"Ah, way before our time, I'm sorry, we only bought the place a few weeks ago. This is our first season." She raised her eyebrows. "I can give you the details for the agent, I think he knew the woman who sold us the place quite well. He might know where she went." She scrolled through her phone and passed on the number.

"Thanks, Miranda. You've been helpful."

She drove away from the bay and up to the row of shops, where the estate agent was. There was a shop which sold buckets and spades next door, and a bakery, which would probably have sold her a much nicer pasty than she had for lunch. The estate agent sat up a little straighter when she walked in.

"Can I help?" His hair flopped over one eye and he pushed it back.

"I'm with the police." She held out her warrant card. "I'm looking for the previous owner of this address, I understand you were involved in the sale, and might know where the sellers went to."

"Yes, of course." He checked the address.

"I'm looking for Michael Spencer."

"Mike. Well, I haven't seen him in years. He used to be a partner in the company that ran the property. It's a holiday let business. The property though, belonged to the other partner in the business. They were also a couple. Mike left years ago, I think he left her in a bad position, moneywise. But she moved locally. I can give you her new address." He wrote on a pad, and passed it over to her.

"Hang on. Is this a rebuild? Is she living in a glorified garden shed?"

"Yes. Is it a problem?"

"No, it's all fine. Thanks for your help." She took the address from him, and pushed open the door into the street.

21.

Julia sat on the bed, and realized that she was on her own, for the first time in a while. She had agreed to donate the stem cells, on a couple of conditions, which Florian and the doctors had agreed. It seemed very fast, from agreeing to sitting here, waiting for the doctor to set up the equipment. They had explained, it would be a minor thing for her. It was the next step that she was concentrating on. She had been so angry with Florian, and then she had, somewhere on the journey, begun to feel a little sorry for him, or perhaps she had just got to know him as a person. He was annoying, and there was something hidden, behind the face he showed to the world, but was that just how a lot of people felt about their brother? She took a breath and closed her eyes, and thought about her mothers, both of them.

Since she had sat by the bed of her frail, helpless birth mother, she had been running through her mind how her real Mum would have felt about this meeting. She had always been very keen on doing the right thing, she had pushed Julia to volunteer for community work and, as a teenager, it had been the thing she resented, but she had enjoyed it and learned from it. Her Mum would have done the right thing, of that she was sure. Had she done the right thing in taking Julia from her father? If he was as much of a criminal as Florian said, maybe that was exactly what she did.

"Julia?" The doctor from earlier stood by the bed in scrubs. "We're good to go." He fitted a canular in both arms and set up the equipment around her. "OK. As we discussed, the blood will be taken out of this arm, we will extract the part we need, and then the rest will go back into the other arm. You will need to be here for about four hours, but we will check in on you regularly, and bring you cups of tea and so on." He checked the canular and the tubes. "What you are doing will save her life. It's a great gift to be able to give your mother." He left her to it and she was pleased to have the peace to think about it all.

She closed her eyes and she saw Ben and Mick. She had known that once she phoned Ben and let him know where she was, there was no chance that she could help her mother. The police would be here and it would stop everything. She had taken the decision to help, and then, she would go, and see Ben and find out what had happened to her dog. She knew he was safe, he couldn't be in a better place than with a vet. She smiled to herself when she thought of Ben. She had been on her own for a long time. Since Mike left, she had been wary of trusting men, and, she had been too busy rebuilding the business and paying back the debts he had left her with. It had been hard work, and what little time she had to herself she wanted to spend with her friends. Perhaps once the house was built, she would have a bit more time. She took a breath and promised herself she would make time for Ben. If he was interested. Which he might be. She closed her eyes again and concentrated on her breathing like Lou had shown her.

Nurses came in with tea and then later with a sandwich. The blood kept coming out of her and going back in. She read three magazines and two pamphlets on diseases she hoped never to have, before closing her eyes again and drifting off to sleep.

A gentle hand on her arm woke her as the light faded, and she opened her eyes. A nurse was smiling down at her, and the donation was complete. They removed the canula and she stood to stretch out her stiff back.

"Where are you going tonight? You'll need to rest for a few days before you go back to work." She packed away the equipment. "I like your Mum, she's very sweet, but a bit sad." She turned to Julia. "She really perked up when you got here. Your brother has been very good with her over the last couple of years, but she is so excited that you're here. You've made such a difference to her."

"Thank you." Julia smiled. "I live in Cornwall, so if she needs another donation, can I give it there?"

"It might be possible, perhaps we can work it out. Your contact details are on her notes, so they would contact you direct, but you will be talking to your Mum anyway, won't you?" Something changed in the nurse's face. Curiosity? Disapproval?

"That really isn't up to me." Julia smiled slowly. That was exactly true. She walked out of the hospital, and walked to the tube station. The evening was cool and she was glad of the hoodie she pulled around her. The tube took her to Paddington, and she caught a late train which trundled through the dark to Plymouth. She tried to remember the last time she had caught the train. It had been years. The gentle swaying motion soothed her though and she watched the lights through the window. She knew that things would swing in to action once she phoned people, but that could wait. She was in limbo and it was quite a comfortable place to be, so she could catch her breath before she made the call. She had made some decisions, and they were clear in her head. She felt relaxed enough to let the train carry her home.

In her bag were the deeds to the house where she had grown up, and a necklace with her name on it, both gifts from a father she had never known, who had been living in Cornwall, perhaps even close to her. It had been a strange couple of days. She had left Florian and her mother with her stem cells, and some decisions to make. She might never hear from them again.

"Good evening, we will shortly be arriving at Plymouth, that's Plymouth. If you will be leaving us at this station, please make sure that you take all your personal possessions with you, and I would like to wish you a safe and pleasant onward journey." The crackle of the announcement was friendly and she thought about her onward journey. She picked up her bag and waited by the door as the train lurched to a stop.

The door opened and she stepped out on to the platform. She climbed the stairs to the exit, and found a public phone which worked. She looked up the number for the vets and dialled.

"Hello?" It was good to hear Ben's voice.

"Ben? Hi. It's Julia."

"Julia! Where are you?"

"I'm at Plymouth station. I'm fine. It's all been a bit of a nightmare, but it's sorted now." She slumped against the wall.

"I'll come and get you. Don't put the phone down." She could hear him rattling keys and grabbing things, before running down the stairs.

"I phoned the vets, not your mobile." She smiled into the phone.

"It's OK, it's diverted to my mobile. I'm coming to get you. Keep talking to me. What happened to you? Where have you been?" She heard the door of the car slam.

"I've been with my brother. I met my mother, and I found out about my father. It has been exhausting. I went to London. I've caught the train back."

"You met your mother? Oh wow. How did that go?"

"It was strange, and great and sad and happy and really weird. It would have been better I think if she spoke better English or I understood her better. But it was good to meet her. It felt like something I should do." She closed her eyes and waited.

"I can see how that would be. I suppose. Are you safe though? You're OK?"

"Yes, I'm just tired. Ben, you don't have to come, I can get a taxi, if you like."

"Don't be silly. I'm already on the way. I've got loads to tell you. The Police have been out looking for you. I chased the van, I thought you were in danger. It was really scary. Hang on a minute, right that's OK. I know Gemma has been looking all over the place for you, Devon and Dorset Police too. I don't know how they didn't find you." He took a breath. "I've been so worried. Well, we all have. Jamie phoned, the guys were really worried about what happened. He said they missed you on the team. They carried on. He said the roof is all done and the first of the windows should arrive tomorrow. Oh, and I got a text from Hugo. His bar is doing really well, he's loving it over there."

"Ben, please!"

"Sorry? What did I say?"

"It's what you didn't say, please tell me." She swallowed a sob. "Is Mick dead?" She swiped a tear from her eye. "Did he die without me there?"

"No. Julia. Please stop crying. Please listen to me, can you hear me? He's alive. He woke a few hours after you left. He's eating and drinking. He's putting up with dog food, and wanting to get back to eating proper dinners with you."

"He's alive?" She cried louder. "Ben? Did you say he's alive?" Her tears and the sobs ripped through her, and she sat down on the floor. "God, I've been telling myself that he died without me there, without me telling him how much he meant to me. I thought I'd let him down. Is he OK, were there any after effects from the poison?"

"He's fine. He's been out for a walk with me today and our receptionist has been spoiling him rotten. Don't cry. He knows he's important. He just misses you. I think he misses your shed too." He laughed, a strange noise, like a cough and a hiss. "I've been telling him you were coming home soon, and that he had to get strong and wait for you. I'm fairly sure that he was listening to me. I hope so anyway."

"Oh! Oh! I can't wait to see him. How far away are you? I'll start walking towards you now, so it's quicker." She stood up, and wiped her tears.

"No. Please don't. I can't bear to lose you again. I mean. Sorry, I mean, it might mean it takes longer." She stood still and listened to his discomfort, and felt her pulse in her neck against the phone.

"How far away are you? How long?" She heard herself asking the question, without having thought about it first.

"I'm pulling off the main road now. I'll be there soon. Don't, please go wandering anywhere."

"I'm not going anywhere." She stood holding the phone, and waiting, as he drove into the pull in area in front of the station, she saw the car pull up. "I see you. I see you." She put the phone down and picked up her bag, and walked out of the station. He opened the door and stepped out, as she walked towards him across the tarmac. He lurched forwards nearly losing his footing, as Mick forced his way through, bounding out of the car and crossing the distance between them in two leaps. She crouched, and then knelt as he wagged his tail so wildly his whole body shook and twisted. He yelped and whined and barked. His whole body and face were so filled with joy. Tears streamed down her face, her arms wrapped around the warm furry body. It took time for the dog to calm down. On the journey home he lay across her lap, and she stroked his head. "If I knew I would get this kind of welcome, I would have come home sooner." She whispered into his silky ears. "Best boy. I'm sorry I wasn't there when you woke up. I'm so sorry." She leaned forwards to tap Ben on the shoulder. "Thank you so much for this."

"For picking you up?"

"Yes, but for fixing Mick, for looking after him, for worrying about me. All of it."

"You're welcome." He smiled at the road ahead, and she watched it in the mirror.

"Would you like a coffee?"

"I would."

"I have some at the shed, provided Jamie's team didn't drink it all." She laughed. "We're going home Mickey boy." She ruffled his ears and he lolled against her.

"That sounds great." He drove up to the gate and she hopped out to open it. Mick jumped out of the car and walked up into the long grass. He parked the car, and they walked towards her little shed. Mick sniffed and checked and followed them. As they got nearer, he caught her hand as it swung between them, slowing her. She turned to him, and he leaned down, his face just an inch from hers. His hand slipped up to cup her face, and she raised herself on tiptoe to meet his lips with hers. It was soft and slow and sparked heat and soft melting in her belly that spread upwards to her throat and to her arms and legs. She reached up and stroked his neck.

"This is nice. I'm feeling very welcomed home." She smiled against his lips. "Come on, lets get that coffee." She left her hand in his and they walked up to the shed. Mick ran in through the door, and gladly accepted a biscuit, before he lay down on the rug.

"Julia?" He wrapped his arms around her, and the warmth of him against her body was mesmerizing. Her knees buckled, perhaps tiredness from the last few days. Or just raw need. It had been such a long time. His mouth grazed hers. His breath was hot on her neck. She felt her spine stretch and her head drop back on her shoulders. "Julia. I, I am so glad to have you back here." His hands felt huge on her back. "Please don't disappear again." He tipped her head back up, to look her in the eyes. "You ok with this?"

She slid her hand up his body, to the side of his face. "Yes." Her mouth met his. Her eyes flickered closed and she leaned into his body. He ran both hands down from her shoulders, towards her hands.

"What's this?" His finger rested on the plaster where the canula had been. "And this?" On the other arm too.

"I gave a stem cell donation. That's why my brother came to get me. My Mother needed a donation. He wasn't a match, I was. So, I donated." He pulled back from her, his face clouded and his eyebrows knitting together. "It was my choice. I spoke to the doctors. I agreed. She won't die now."

"When were you going to tell me this?" He moved away from her. "He came and grabbed you, Julia, I saw it, I watched you thrown into the back of his van. I chased the van. I couldn't find you. You disappeared for two days. You were sitting calmly in a hospital, and you didn't phone me or the police? Oh no, no, no. I have to phone Gemma and let her know you're back. I totally forgot. Damn." He pulled his phone out of his pocket.

"I'm not pressing charges against my brother. I understand why he did it. I got to know him a little more, and I think to understand him a bit. I made some conditions before I gave my donation, and he has stuck to them, at least, so far. This is a big deal for me. I had no family at all last week, now all of a sudden, I have a father, who lives near here. A Mother who is alive but sick, and a brother." His finger hovered over the screen on his phone. "I know you have to tell them, but please let me explain to them, I want the chance to get to know my family. Please?" Her hands reached out for him. "I would have told you about it anyway. I was just so happy that Mick was OK, and you came to get me from the Station. It's been a tough couple of days to get my head around."

"OK. I won't say anything but that you're back. You'll have to take it from there." He shook his head. "Gemma's alright, she's a friend of mine, sort of. You can talk to her." She turned away from him and filled the kettle. "Hi. Gemma? She's back. Fine, safe and sound." There was a pause. "Yes, thank you, so relieved. Yes, she'll be there. OK thanks, and thanks for all you did. Bye." He took the coffee cup she offered. "She says to tell you welcome home, and she wants to see you in the morning, to go through everything. I can take you to the station if you like."

"Thanks Ben. For not saying what you think, I mean." She sipped her coffee. The shed was small, but it seemed there was a huge gap between them.

"Well, thanks for the coffee. Micks OK, but keep an eye on him, just in case. He will be a bit weaker than before for a while. I'd better get going." He put down the cup and stepped towards the door.

"Please don't go." It was almost a whisper. He turned back and looked at her.

"How can I stay, when you don't trust me enough to tell me the truth?" His hand was still on the handle of the door.

"I'll tell you all of it. It's not I don't trust you, it's more that I haven't processed it in my own head yet." She reached out her hand. "Come and sit down. Telling you might help me to work out what happened." He hesitated, but his hand met hers and they sat down. Him on the only chair and her on the bed. She sipped her coffee, and told the story of how she had made the journey up to London, and what she had learned about her father. How hurt she had been when she realized that Florian had taken her to get a donation from her, how the tiny bird like woman who had her eyes and her chin, had been so completely sure Julia would save her, and finally, how she had made a deal with Florian, not to report his abduction of her, but that he would stay away, while she gave the donation and afterwards. She would be going home. If her mother needed another donation, she would give it, but she would not hear from either of them unless they were ready to be a family, and tell the truth. If the donation was all they wanted, that was fine, but be honest about it, she had told him. Unless you want to make a real go of being a family. He had agreed and thanked her, and she had left the hospital after the procedure and caught a train home.

His eyes held hers. "Do you think they will come looking for you again?"

She wiped her hand over her eyes. "I don't know. I have given them the perfect way out if all they wanted was my stem cells. I suppose we wait and see." Mick snored in the corner. "Are you tired?"

"Yes. I know you were here yesterday, but it felt like a month." He rubbed his hand across his eyes. "You've been through a lot of stuff. I get how it would turn you inside out. My family are so completely normal and boring, for which I am grateful, right now." He chuckled.

"Lie down. At least let's get some rest, and tomorrow, I'll sort all this out with Gemma, and get everything back to normal. I want to find out more about my father though. It's weird that he lives near here, I mean I might have met him, or at least seen him, and not known he was my father." She pulled the pillow straight and then tucked it between her neck and her shoulder.

Ben hesitated but only for a second. "I suppose it's possible. I might know him too, if he lived locally, just to say hello to, perhaps." He pushed his boots off, and lay down beside her. Her face was inches away. Her hands curled around each other in front of her chest. Her eyes met his, and held. He reached for her waist and wrapped his arm around her. His face moved closer and his lips gently found hers.

Slowly and carefully his body and hers found their way around each other. Discovering and testing like a taster menu, each kiss and stroke, measured against the other's reaction. No rush or pressure, just searching for each other, and slowly but surely, finding where they wanted to be, and where they had known all along, they would each find the other.

22.

"Thanks for coming in." Gemma pushed a very bad cup of tea across the desk towards Julia. She had heard the story, or the parts of it that Julia had decided to tell. Gemma knew she was leaving things out, but that was a problem for another time. There were more pressing issues to deal with. "I have some other questions I need to go through with you. Is that OK?" Julia nodded. "Do you know a man called Michael Spencer?"

"Yes. Well, I used to. We moved down here together. I bought the property, but we owned the business together. We were doing alright, but he insisted we needed to do up the buildings, so we took out a loan. The next day he took the money out of our business account and left. He left a letter to say he was resigning as a Director, and I never saw him again. That was, five years ago, no a bit longer perhaps." Julia tried the tea and put it back down.

"OK, do you know anyone by the name of Alex? Or Mr Alex?" Gemma opened a folder in front of her, when Julia shook her head. "Have a look at this photograph." She slid it across the desk. "It's a bit grainy, but I think you can make it out."

"Oh, yes, I know him. He used to come to the beach in the mornings, at Constantine Bay. I used to swim there every morning, and he would be there, having a coffee or just sitting, looking at the view or something. He would say 'hello' or whatever, but I didn't know his name." Julia thought back to the beach in the mornings, and the old man who always had a smile and a friendly greeting. "I always thought, or maybe I was wrong, but I always felt he was waiting for someone."

"Right, but do you remember seeing him with anyone else?" Gemma leaned on the desk.

"No, I don't think so." She chewed her lip gently, her eyes half closed while she searched through her memories. "I thought at one time, that he was watching Amanda, my friend, but she's very bright and bubbly, the sort of girl men do watch, if you know what I mean?"

"OK. So, he was there alone, and you said hello, and then what?"

"I would usually get back into my car and go home. Sometimes I had a coffee, there was a little place there. Amanda liked to have a coffee there on the way into work, sometimes I'd stop and have one with her, or when Lou was working in the hotel down there, she'd sometimes pop down to catch up. That was a few years ago now, when they had the spa there. They knew I'd be there in the mornings, I liked it then, it was quieter." She pushed her hair out of her face.

"What did your brother tell you about when he met your father?" Gemma pushed the photograph back into the folder.

"Not much, he said he met him and he told Florian where my, um Janice who brought me up, lived. I don't think he said anything else. He gave me a necklace that our Father had bought for me, and the deeds to the house I told you about. My Brother didn't know my father either, but he had tracked him down to find out if he knew where I was. It was me he was looking for, I explained earlier." Julia checked her memory of what Florian had said.

"It appears that we have found Mr Spencer. He left, as you said, having removed money from your business bank account. He had planned to move to Tintagel, he had rented a property there, but he never arrived. We found his body, buried in a shallow grave just a few miles away from where you lived before. We believe that he was murdered, and his body was disposed of there." Gemma watched her face.

"Oh. Mike's dead?" Her breath caught on a small sob. "All these years, I thought he had stolen the money and gone, dumped me in it. Someone made him do it, take the money, I mean?"

"No. The money is in his bank account still, untouched. His wallet, with cash and credit cards was buried with him." Gemma waited.

"So, why then? Why kill him?"

"I don't know, I hoped you might be able to tell me about him, maybe help me work out why?"

"I'll tell you whatever I can, but honestly, I had no clue he was about to take the money and go, it was a shock. I did think he had been a bit restless, unhappy for a while, maybe a few months? Like he was irritated a lot of the time and grumpy, but I just thought Mike was being Mike, and I didn't get into it. I wondered afterwards." She looked straight at Gemma. "I mean I thought there was probably someone else."

"Did you suspect anyone you knew, or you just thought there must be someone because he left?"

"I, thought there must be. He was always so worried about money, feeling like unequal because I bought the property, always wanting designer stuff and a flash car and all that sort of stuff. I wasn't fussed. I like nice things, who doesn't? But not like him, he was desperate, like money made him more confident or better or something."

"What did you do, when he left?"

"I went to work, did up the properties myself, and paid back the loan. I had his letter, so I took his name off the company, and worked hard, to build the business."

"You didn't report him missing?"

"Why would I? He had resigned and left. I had his letter." She chewed her lip. "I always thought it was strange he didn't pop up again. You know, bump into old friends, and them saying, I saw Mike the other day, or whatever. I thought perhaps they were being kind, not telling me to spare my feelings, particularly if he had turned up with a girl." She shrugged. "Do you think he was moving to Tintagel with someone?"

"If he was, then nobody else knew about it. The house was rented in his name, and the agents only met him."

"Do you think he was coming back? If he hadn't been killed, I mean?"

"I have no way of knowing. I am going to ask around your friends, and see if they knew anything at the time, and, like you say, didn't mention it to you, in case it upset you. I need to contact your brother, too, do you have an address for him, or your mother?"

"No. I have a mobile number for Florian, I can give you that." She pulled her phone out of her bag and scrolled through. Yes, here it is. She pushed the phone across the desk so Gemma could copy the number.

"Are you still in touch with Florian?"

"No. I told him not to contact me again, unless he was ready to be totally truthful and be a proper family."

"What do you think he's being untruthful about?"

"I don't know, but I know there's something. I think, from what he said, my father was a bit of a villain, but some of that could be because he's angry that he left them. It just feels like he's holding something back. He almost admitted that he's not been entirely honest with me. So, I will wait and either I will hear from them, or I won't." She shrugged, but it was clearly not easy to shake these feelings off. "It's a bit like putting your life in a blender. I have a family, I don't, I do." She took a deep breath and let it go.

"OK. I'll be in touch with you shortly. Meantime, take care of yourself." Gemma reached across the desk and patted her arm.

The day outside was sunny and the sky was the wide blue that brought people back year after year to Cornwall. Julia breathed a sigh and walked to her Land Rover. Mick sat patiently on the passenger seat, waiting to wag and yelp his joy at her return.

23.

"Hey! You're finally here. Thank God. The tea seems of have dried up." Jamie slung an arm around her shoulder. "We finished the roof. The windows just arrived for upstairs, and for the skylights. They should be mostly in today." He was walking with her to the shed. "Ben called and told me he would personally do me damage if I let you work today, so your duties are entirely tea related." He smiled down into her face. "OK mate?"

"OK. I bought cake and extra biscuits though, it would be a shame not to share." She left him to carry on and put on the kettle. Mick seemed to be sticking a little closer to her, not running off to the woods for a sniff like he usually did. Together they made the tea, and she carried it out, along with cake, and passed it around. Mick had a dog chew and they all sat on the grass.

She gazed up at the house, and the new roof. It was all coming together, and soon, really soon, she would have a proper home. Inheriting the house in London had changed things too. She couldn't imagine living there, but knowing it was there, and safe, was a good feeling. It was good to sit and have tea with the guys too. She had only been missing for a day, but it felt longer.

She spent an hour lying on her bed, and then sat on the steps for a little while with Mick. "Come on, Mick." They walked across to the gate and she leaned on the top rail. "Doesn't look like anyone's coming boy." She leaned down and rubbed her hand across his head. "Shall I make us some pasta, boy?" His tongue lolled out of his mouth, which she took as agreement.

"Hey, Julia, come and see." Jamie called her. She walked up the driveway and stood outside the house. "Look, look! He pulled open the front door and stood on the drive with her. "You have a door!" He danced a little bit and smiled a lot. She looked down the side of the house, where glass glinted in the sun. "Come on, come and see the best bit." He led her around to the other side of the house, which faced the view she had fallen in love with on her first visit. "Ta da." He spread his hand in an arc, like a magician, and there, better than she had imagined, was the wall of glass, stretching from the ground to the roof line. She would be able to stand in her living room, or in her bedroom and see her view, in all weathers, at all times of the day or night. It was her view completely.

"Jamie. Oh, thank you Jamie. It's better than I imagined. It's perfect. Thank you. Look Mick. We have windows!" She jumped up and down. Mick jumped around her.

"We're packing up, but we'll be here in the morning, before the rest of the windows arrive. Are you OK, really?" He watched her closely.

"Yup. I'm just a bit tired. I'm going to walk the dog and then get an early night. I'll be ready to watch you work tomorrow morning." She watched the clouds scud across the sky reflected in her beautiful window. "Really good windows, Jamie." He waved as he walked away, and she waved too.

Her phone rang and she pulled it out of her pocket. "Hi Ben."

"Hello, how are you? Sorry I couldn't ring earlier. I had an emergency. How did it go with Gemma?"

"OK, I think, except, well she told me some things I didn't know, strange stuff. I'll tell you all about it when I see you."

"When can I see you?"

"Whenever you are free. Jamie put some of the windows in

today, it looks amazing. When you have time, come and have a look." She listened, he sounded as though he was struggling with something. "You OK?"

"Yeah, just fighting with a gate, one handed." He huffed. "OK, I'll see you soon then?"

"OK. I was just about to start cooking, are you hungry?" But she was too late. He had hung up. She shrugged her shoulders and went back to watching the sky reflected in her new window. Mick's yelps and little barks made her look. Ben was walking up the driveway with a pizza box and a bottle of wine, looking very pleased with himself. "Hello, I didn't know you did deliveries. Ha ha, just realized, you were fighting with my gate, weren't you?" He wrapped his arm around her and pulled her close. "What do you think of my windows?" He turned to look.

"Wow. They look amazing. And the view will be fantastic. Oh, Julia, this is better than I imagined." He leaned down to kiss her and she closed her eyes, knowing that this was better than she could have imagined.

"I'll get some glasses, and feed the dog, we can have a picnic here, if you like?" He nodded and watched her go, followed by Mick. She was back a few minutes later with glasses, and a rug, which she threw on the grass. Mick loped behind her sat next to her. They ate the pizza and drank the wine, while she told him most of what had happened with Gemma. "There are a couple of things she told me that I didn't know about though." He nodded, and waited. "They found a body, well, Mike Spencer's body to be exact. He ran out on me and our business having emptied the bank account, and left me in a mess. I thought he would have gone back to London, but apparently not. He had rented a place in Tintagel, but never turned up, because he was dead. All the years I spent worrying that he would come back, or waiting for a friend to say, they'd bumped into him, or whatever, and he was already dead." She sipped her wine. "It's strange, I've been angry with him a long time, but I would never have wanted him hurt.

Feels weird. Also, they asked me about a guy I'd never heard of, Alex something, but they showed me a picture. I recognized him, he used to be at the beach a lot in the mornings when I swam there."

"Mr Alex?" Ben sat forward.

"Yes, that's right, that was what she said."

"What connection is he to you?"

"I don't know. Like I say, he used to say hello, or good morning or something, and I would say hello back. That's it. Why, do you know him?" She put her arm around the dog, his warm weight was comfortable.

"I do. Mr Alex is a customer, and he was Mick's owner." He looked from her to the dog.

"But you said he was missing." Her brows

"Yes. I did." He nodded.

"So, she thinks there's a connection between them and me." Her eyes searched side to side. "Did someone I know kill Mike? Oh no. Does she think I killed him?"

"No. I'm sure she doesn't think that. Let me have a chat with her tomorrow and see if I can find out more. OK? It's most likely completely unrelated." He moved his arm, to wrap it around her, and Mick nuzzled his hand. They were quiet as the clouds turned pink and the sun dipped towards the hills. "It's getting a bit chilly out here isn't it?"

"Yes. Let's get a coffee to warm us up." She gathered up the rug and the empty glasses and he took the rest. Mick trotted off into the grass, but not far away.

24.

"Hi. Something's been niggling me, did you say there was a letter from a hotel in the paperwork you found, something about leaving something behind or not finding something?" She was already on her third coffee. She could tell her phone call had woken him, but she was unworried by that.

"Boss? Um, yes. There was a letter. A hotel up the coast a bit. I thought it was odd because, why would anyone stay in a hotel so close to home."

"Where, up the coast?"

"Oh, Tintagel."

"Right. Get dressed and into work. I want you to come with me today. We have stuff to do." She hung up before he could answer. Her phone rang again. "Hello Ben."

"Hi Gemma. Sorry to bother you at work. It's just that I saw Julia last night and she told me that you found the body of her ex. I just want to know if she's safe? Is there someone out there killing people around her?" He was breathing a little too deeply, and she could hear it.

"I don't know. I am fairly sure she's in no danger, but until I work out what happened I don't know for sure. I have some stuff to follow up, and then maybe we'll know more. It might not be a bad idea to keep an eye out for the brother though. I don't see any reason why he would hurt her, given that he had an opportunity to, and didn't. He has a past, though. I am telling you this off the record. Do not repeat it, not even to Julia. He is known to police in Manchester, but they haven't been able to get him on anything." She took a sip of her coffee.

"Right, thank you. I won't say anything. Thanks for the warning." She hung up.

Gemma was ready to go, when he arrived. They left the station, once he had found the letter, and drove up the coast to Tintagel. The hotel was in the main street, across the road from Merlin's Kitchen. It smelled nice, and the receptionist was very welcoming. Gemma introduced herself, and the manager was called.

"I understand this is about a letter?"

"Yes." Gemma pushed it across the desk in the Manager's very sumptuous office. She was in her early fifties, well groomed, expensive looking. "I need to know more about this letter, what was left behind, and when this gentleman stayed here." The Manager's heavily extended eyelashes drifted towards the screen on her desk.

"Right, Mr Alex, yes, there are a couple of letters, he wrote asking if he left his umbrella, we had a look, nothing had been handed in or found by housekeeping, so we wrote back saying no. He stayed with us a few times. I'll print off the dates for you." She hit a key with a long, polished nail and the printer whirred.

"Can you check if Michael Spencer stayed here around the same time?" Gemma waited.

"Yes, here he is, oh he was here a lot, with Mrs Spencer. I'll print those dates off too."

Gemma left, armed with the printed dates. She felt scruffy in comparison with the room and the woman she had just left. It made her feel defensive.

"Right. I'll shout you a coffee, and then we'll go through those dates. I want to know if they were there at the same time." She passed him the paperwork and gave him the keys to the car, while she bought two coffees and a couple of Danish pastries. She hoped by the time she got back to the car he would have the answer, and he did not disappoint.

"Both times, they were there, both times. The second time Mr Alex was there was the last time both of them were there. Oh, thank you. Just what I needed." He took a sip of the coffee. "If they were all there, at the same time, then Julia would have known Mr Alex, or at least would have recognized him from there. It seems unlikely that they would be there twice at the same time unless it was arranged."

"If it was Julia. Maybe he was with another woman, which was why he was in a hotel in the first place?" She took a small bite of the pastry. "But I think you're right, whether Julia was there or not, this all seems to revolve around her."

"So perhaps he was moving to Tintagel to be with this other woman? If she exists."

"That's a good point." Gemma sipped her coffee and looked at her nails. They were tidy, and short. No polish. "Julia did say she thought he might have been having an affair, but, if someone leaves you, I suppose you would think that, wouldn't you?"

"Yes, maybe you could read stuff into situations that wasn't there. I can see that." He licked his fingers, and sipped his coffee.

"I think we have to talk to Julia again. Did tech have any luck with his phone?"

"I'll check in with them. We're waiting for some stuff from the lab too." He picked up his phone and dialled.

She drove while he talked, and she watched the weather change from cloudless blue to heavy clouds, throwing rain at the car as she wound her way along the coast road, and back to rain washed blue. This was what she loved about Cornwall, the way it could change and surprise you at every turn of the road. He was still talking to the lab on the phone and she tuned him out.

She gave herself time, to think about Michael Spencer, and why he had been at a hotel. Julia had seemed shocked. She had seen enough people who were faking shock before, to recognize the real thing. She needed evidence though, her belief was really not enough. There was a feeling, a worrying worm of a feeling, that this was spiralling out of control. She had done some digging into Mr Alex, which was not his real name, but he was certainly very well known to the London police, in connection with drugs, and several murders, but with no convictions. He had, they believed, been involved at a very high level, but again there was no proof. Florian was a similar case. He was known to be working with drug supply at a high level in Manchester, but without proof, there was nothing they could do.

She pulled up outside Julia's gate, and told him to follow her when he was finished on the phone. She pushed the gate closed behind her and walked up the driveway.

"Julia?" She watched her turn at the sound of her name. "Hi. Have you got a minute to talk?"

"Yes. Of course. Do you want a tea or something?" She called the dog, and he loped across the grass towards her. Together the three of them walked to the shed. She watched Julia fill the kettle and waited.

"I wanted to know. Did you ever go to a hotel in Tintagel? The Cornishman Inn?" Julia thought about it.

"I went to Tintagel with the girls once, we stayed at a hotel that looked like a castle. I don't remember the name of it, but I've got a feeling it was something to do with Camelot or something. It was only for a weekend, for Lou's birthday, I think. It was a few years ago." She passed a cup to Gemma.

"Did you ever go there with Mike Spencer?"

"No. If we went away for a weekend we usually went to London, to catch up with friends up there." She drank from her cup.

"OK. That's fine. I just wanted to check." She sat down. "How are you feeling?"

"I'm fine. I have my lovely dog, and Ben is popping in to see me from time to time. The builders are cracking on with the house, as you can hear. Everything's good. I haven't heard from my brother, or my birth Mother, which is OK, but a bit sad. I'm fine." She leaned against the little table which served as a kitchen.

"Ah, Hello. This is my Sergeant." They both watched the young man cross the grass towards them.

"Hello. Sorry boss, can I have a quick word?" Gemma stepped out of the shed and they put their heads together. Nodding heads and quick conversations. Gemma nodded at him and they both came back into the shed. It was crowded with all of them inside.

"Julia. I have some news. First of all, we did a DNA test on you, remember? We also ran a test on a blood test a local doctor had taken from the man we know as Mr Alex. It seems very, very likely that he was your father." Gemma watched her reaction very carefully.

"My Father? Why didn't he tell me? He used to say hello in the mornings. Once he told me he was sitting on the beach so he didn't have cake with a coffee. I should have talked to him more. I wish I had got to know him. Any idea where he went to?" Her eyebrows furrowed together.

"I don't know. I am trying to find out as much as I can about him, but it's a bit patchy still. I am going to level with you. If Florian comes down to see you again, I want to talk to him. I want to find out what happened when he met your father. There's something else."

"Oh. OK, go on then."

"We found a phone in Mike Spencer's bag. It was damp, and there was very little we could get from it, but we have spoken to the provider, and got a list of the calls and texts he sent and received. I can tell you that he was having a relationship with someone else. I don't know if that helps or makes it worse." She watched the expression on Julia's face, either she was a fantastic actress, or she genuinely had been unsure before.

"How big was the place he was moving to in Tintagel?"

"Sorry?"

"A bedsit? A four-bedroom house?" Julia put down her cup. "I mean, was it only him?"

"There were three bedrooms and a large garden." Julia lifted her eyebrows.

"Right. So, he expected her to move with him, whoever she was." She nodded. "I wonder what she thought when he didn't turn up. She must have been waiting somewhere. That's a bit sad."

"I suppose. I should tell you, his body was found buried on your Father's land." Julia's eyes snapped wide open.

"What? My Father's land? How did that happen?" Julia's hands flew to her face. "How did they even know each other?" She took a breath heavily. "It's like I've been living my life with everything hidden. How could I not know all this stuff?"

"If people lie to you, and you trust them, why would you know the truth?" Gemma put her hand on Julia's arm. "Trusting people is normal. It's not your fault that people are dishonest. I need to find out what happened, and who was involved. I have a murder to solve, and a missing person to find, and I need you to help me when I ask you. I will tell you as much as I can as we go along, OK?"

Back at her desk, she sifted through the paperwork, again. There was always more you could learn, and at the moment, this was all she had. The hospital where Julia had met her mother had an address, which turned out to be a fast food restaurant, and at the moment that was the only lead she had for Florian or his Mother.

Their mobile numbers were switched off. She came to the print out from the hotel. It showed the date, the breakfast booking, which room they had stayed in, and a booking reference. WRP. What did it mean? Maybe nothing, but it was worth double checking.

"Hello, we spoke the other day, about Mr Spencer and his booking at your hotel?"

"Oh yes, hello."

"Just a quick question, on the print out you gave me, the booking reference, WRP what does that mean?"

"Oh, website remote payment." She paused. "It means it was booked on the website, and payment was made through the site, not at reception. Some people prefer to do that."

"Can you tell me if Mr Spencer made the booking himself, or was it someone else?" Gemma was hopeful. Another name, another somebody to chase.

"Give me a moment." She could hear tapping in the background. "Yes, I can, Ms Burton made the booking, not Mr Spencer."

"Do you have a home address?"

"Yes. It's The Copper Beeches, Staunton Lane, Constantine Bay."

"Thank you. Very much." Gemma hung up, and picked up her keys. The other woman was local. Julia might know her, that would be a reason to be out of the area. She picked up her coat and went to the car.

The house was huge. Beautiful, very old and very well kept, the gardens were shaped and clipped, and everything looked expensive. Gemma pushed down the feelings that her scruffy appearance was putting her at a disadvantage and rang the bell. Something chimed far away.

"Yes?" The girl who opened the door looked to be in her late teens.

"Is Ms Burton at home?" Gemma flashed her warrant card.

"Um, yeah. Come in." She moved backwards to open the door. "Mum! Police here for you." She shouted up the stairs and left Gemma standing in the hall.

Footsteps down the staircase were light and fast. "Hello?"

"Ms Burton?"

"Yes." Gemma held out her warrant card again, and the woman batted it away. "What's happened?"

"I need to ask you some questions, about a booking you made at the Cornishman Inn in Tintagel, some time ago now. Do you remember it?" The woman sat, abruptly on the stairs. Gemma had time to look at her carefully, she was thin, and as well maintained as the house. Good hair and sharp looking nails.

"Oh." She reached for the bannister and pulled herself up. "Come into the living room, we can talk in there." Gemma followed her through a huge doorway, and they sat on a squashy sofa. "It was a few years ago. I was going through a bad patch, with my husband, with my life, really. I needed a little time away, so I took myself off to a hotel for a break."

"But you booked the room in the name of Mr Michael Spencer?" Gemma watched a flicker at the side of the woman's eye.

"Yes."

"Why would that be?"

"Because, he was one of the reasons I was going through a bad patch." There was irritation in her voice. "Look, I had a fling with him, not for long. I'm not proud of it, but I did. He said he loved me. Said we should run away together." She took a breath. "It was a stupid distraction from some serious problems."

"He rented a house in Tintagel, and left his girlfriend, took money from his business. That would suggest he was ready to leave his life behind. What happened? Did you change your mind?"

"No. I didn't. He did. We had arranged to meet in Tintagel, at the bar in the Cornishman. He never arrived. I waited three hours, then I gave up and went home. I was very hurt. He never contacted me again." She chewed her lower lip.

"Do you know his girlfriend?"

"Yes, I know Julia very well. We've been friends for years. I thought he might come back to her, but he didn't." She studied her hands, and the rings on her fingers for a moment. "Is this going to come out? I mean, my husband doesn't know, and Julia, well, obviously I wouldn't tell her."

"It may do. We have found Mr Spencer's body. This is now a murder investigation, so it may be that your part of his story becomes public."

Her hand flew to her face. "No." Her eyes filled with tears. "I don't believe it."

"If it's any consolation, we think he was on the way to meet you when he was killed."

"Oh. Thank you."

Do you, by any chance, know this man?" She handed over a photo of Mr Alex.

"Yes. He used to have coffee at the beach café most mornings. I don't think I ever spoke to him."

"OK, thank you. I'll let myself out." She nodded, as though she was alone already. Gemma walked out into the hall and opened the front door, pulling it closed behind her.

25.

"I have to go to work." He kissed her again. "I do really have to go, I'd like to stay, and have Jamie and the guys take the mick for the next ten years, about catching me sneaking about in garden sheds, but I'd be late for surgery. I'll call you, later." He kissed her again and this time her arms wrapped around his neck. "Oh. That's not fair."

"Have a lovely day at work." She smiled, feeling sleepy and languid in her bed. He laughed and backed away. She waved and pushed up to sit against the pillows.

He closed the door and she pushed her legs over the edge of the bed, listening to his car door close. She checked the time and pulled some clothes on, before filling the kettle and checking out of the window in time to see Jamie's truck pull in. She giggled. He had been too late. They must have passed each other in the lane. She really didn't understand why he had a problem with people knowing that he had stayed over, they were grown-ups, and single. She shrugged and pulled out more cups. He was a strange mixture of old fashioned and smart very sexy and very kind and there was something hidden in there somewhere that she had yet to work out.

She carried the cups down to the site, and the dog followed her. The guys all grabbed one each, while they watched the windows lorry unload the last of her order. If it all went well, by the end of the day, the house would be weather-proof and they could start on the inside. A bubble of excitement had lodged itself under her ribs. She wanted, really wanted, be able to wake up in that bedroom and see the view.

A car pulled into the driveway, and the policewoman got out.

"Hi. I've just boiled the kettle, would you like one?" Gemma nodded and joined her on the walk back to the shed.

"I have more questions."

"I thought you might." Julia smiled and passed her a cup.

"Do you know Amanda Burton?"

"Amanda? Yes. I met her when we first moved down here. She lives near the bay."

"How well do you know her?"

"She's not my best friend, but we've been out together, girls nights, that sort of thing. Oh my God, was it Amanda having an affair with Mike?"

"It looks that way."

"Shit. What a complete bitch."

"Yes. Probably true."

"She was leaving her husband, and her kids? No. She was going to take her kids with her, that's why the three bedroom house. Tasha would only have been eleven or twelve back then, and Connor, maybe eight. They were going to set up in Tintagel, weren't they, and leave me to pay back the set up money. Bitch. I've sat and talked to her about it, and I had no clue. Well, I feel like a proper idiot." Julia sat on the edge of the bed she had yet to make.

"I think, but I have no proof yet, that your father found out about the affair. He was at the hotel when they were, perhaps he was following them, to find out. Either way, Michael drove to Tintagel, where he had arranged to meet Amanda, and arranged to collect the keys to the house, parked his car in the car park and I think your father intercepted him, and drove him away. I am waiting for a report from forensics, but I think he meant to slap Michael around, angry that he had cheated on you, and it went too far. He buried the body on his land, and got on with his life. It's a theory, I really have very little evidence to back it up. I'm trying to work it out.

"You think my father killed him?" Gemma nodded. "By mistake?"

"Yes. I think so."

"Do you have a theory about why my father has gone missing?"

"Yes. But it has too many holes in it at the moment. I need some facts. Look, I said I'd let you know what happens, and I will, I realize it must be hard to hear all this stuff." She avoided eye contact with Julia.

"It's OK, I won't go round and punch Amanda." Julia huffed out a breath. "Although, it's tempting." She patted Gemma's arm. "It was a long time ago, and I've moved on."

"House is looking good." Gemma watched two men carrying a window inside the house.

"Yeah, I'm pleased with it. I'll need to move in before the winter, and I think that looks possible at the moment."

"Good. OK. I'll let you get on then."

Julia picked up her phone, and answered it on the first ring. "Hi Lou. How's it going?"

"I've got a day off, and I wondered if you had time for a coffee?"

"Yes. Shall I meet you? We can take the dog along the beach for a walk?"

"Great. About ten minutes?"

Julia called Mick to the land rover and set off. She was looking forward to seeing Lou, she was always good fun and she had missed bumping into her for a chat when they lived closer.

The beach was quiet, and Mick was delighted to bound off towards the water. She watched his body, quivering with excitement over each new wave and barking frantically as each wave broke onto the beach, soaking him with salty water.

Coffees bought, they walked along the sand, laughing at Mick's battle with the sea.

"I'm so excited, they said the new Spa would be opening up next week, and they've offered me three days of classes there. It's going to be good money and steady work. It might die off a bit in the winter, but I'll still keep the other classes going for then. So what's been happening with you?" She pushed her hair back out of her face, so she could sip from the coffee cup. The wind whipped it back again. Julia watched her and decided that she wasn't going to say anything about Amanda. It was a long time ago, and life had been too complicated recently, she needed some light happy time with her friend. Not a dire emergency meeting of horrible bitching.

"The house is coming on, you should pop up one evening, and see the place. Oh and I've been seeing Ben, quite a lot." She laughed.

Lou's eyes snapped wide. "Ben, the vet that you called for Mick, when he first arrived? That Ben?"

"Yes, that Ben. He's really nice, you'd like him."

"About time you found someone nice. Good for you, well deserved." Lou wrapped her free arm around Julia's shoulders.

They walked to the big rock at the end of the beach and then turned back. Lou was busy with plans for her new classes, and filled Julia in on the details. Julia was quiet, listening and asking questions. They drew level with the café, and Julia clipped on Mick's lead. He was tired, and dripping sand and sea water. They threw their cups in the huge bin near the tables, and Julia wrapped Lou in a hug.

"It's been great to catch up. Thank you." They turned together to walk up to the car park.

"Julia? Lou?" They recognized Amanda's voice. Julia felt her shoulders stiffen.

"Hi." Lou turned towards Amanda, and gave her a hug. Julia stood back.

"Sorry, wet dog! I think you probably don't want to get too close." Both heads snapped round at the edge in Julia's voice.

"Darling dog, he looks like he had a good time on the beach." Amanda's smile was wide and she waited for Julia to respond. Lou looked from one to the other.

"Yes, he had a lovely time." Julia shook her head, she knew her voice sounded clipped and awkward. "Sorry, got to rush. Take care." She set off with Mick happily trotting beside her, leaving Amanda and Lou behind, watching her go. She had intended to avoid Amanda until this was old news. To see her when it was so raw had been unfortunate. Even the dog was looking surprised at her quick departure.

Her phone rang before she had driven out of the parking area. "Hello."

"Julia?"

"Yes."

"Have I done something to upset you?"

"What do you think? Amanda."

"I think you're upset."

"OK."

"I'm sorry."

"Fuck that." Julia snarled.

"I am sorry though. It was madness. I was stupid and selfish and greedy. Can we get together and talk about this?"

"No. I don't want to talk about it. I really don't. Please stay away from me for a while, so I can get my head straight."

"OK. I am sorry though, and I want to stay friends."

"How? We aren't friends. People who are friends don't do this to each other. You sat and watched me fight my way out of terrifying amounts of debt, which Mike put me in, to be with you. Sleeping with Mike, planning to run away with him, and then watching me pay for it. You're not my friend, or you couldn't have done any of those things. I don't think I could take much more of your kind of friendship. Now please, go away." Julia's hands shook on the steering wheel. More than anything, she wanted to get home, away from this situation. Mick licked a big pink tongue along her arm. She took a breath, and swallowed. On the other end of the phone she could hear Amanda crying. It really didn't make anything better. Her anger made her feel powerless and empty. "Look, I know, you were an idiot. I'm not saying that I've never been a fool, but this is too fresh, too new. Stop crying Amanda. I'm not going to tell anyone else. This is between you and me as far as I am concerned. I don't know where the police are going with it. I just need some space, to be away from you at the moment. OK?"

"Yes. Thank you. I...."

"Please don't tell me that you're sorry again. I think my head would explode. OK. Leave me to be on my own for a bit." Julia hung up the phone and felt hot tears behind her closed eyelids. She felt ashamed, and weak. In the back of her head, she had always imagined that he might have been seeing someone, that he had left her for someone. He had planned it, pushed her into borrowing more money than she was uncomfortable owing, and then taken the money and left her to pick up the pieces while he ran off to have a good time at her expense. Sitting there, in the car park, she understood why her father might have killed him. Right now, knowing how humiliated she had been, that he had slept with her friend, and then the cruelty of leaving her years of paying off the debts, she could have killed him herself.

She started the engine. Her eyes were dry, and her hands were loose on the wheel. She had learned something about herself, in that moment of white-hot rage. She understood why Mike's life had been ended, and she agreed with the decision. Now that the storm had passed, and she was calm again, she felt better. It was a surprise to her, that she was capable of thinking that way. She had always hated violence. She didn't even watch films where people hurt each other. She shook her head.

Her hand stroked across the dog's head. He was still damp around the ears, and now settled on the seat and snored peacefully.

26.

The forensic report was back. Gemma sat at her desk, and read the report, slowly, then again, in case she had missed anything. Michael Spencer's death seemed to have been caused by a gun shot to his head. Small calibre weapon, used at point blank range. There was evidence, although less clear, that he had received a blow to the back of the skull before death which was severe enough, that the bullet was insurance.

Gemma had researched as much as she could, into Mr Alex. He had arrived in the UK as far as she could work out, at the end of the eighties. The file held on him on the Police national database described him as a drug baron, he had a reputation for violence and for his ruthlessness in dealing with anyone who stole from him or owed him money. For years, he had been chased and watched by officers across the force, and he had been arrested over forty times, but never convicted. The witnesses seemed to change their minds or disappear. Then, nothing. He had disappeared. The common belief was that someone had killed him and taken over his business. It seemed that was untrue, and that in actual fact, he had moved to Cornwall, bought a little small holding, and watched over his daughter. Knowing his past, it was a short leap to see that he would not have taken his daughter's humiliation lying down.

Gemma's theory on the murder was starting to come into focus. She had a theory on the disappearance too, that needed work. She needed forensic evidence to tie the suspect to the crime, and then she needed to find all the parties involved.

She drove out to the crime scene again, it had been checked and checked again, but she had to wait for further forensic tests, and until she had the results, she wanted to look around again. The little yard had been cleared, and rain had washed away any evidence of what had happened there. The chicken run was empty and even smelled better now that the animals had been taken away. The house was more orderly now than when they had found it, when it looked as though it had been searched before they got there. Her very methodical sergeant had put the papers into piles and cleared all the surfaces. The book case had been emptied, the books checked and put back, and any documents filed at the station. She would find nothing new in this room, of that she was sure. She walked through to the bedroom. The bed was neatly made, as it had been when they found the property. The corners of the sheets tucked in tightly, and the clothes in the cupboards neatly folded.

The cupboards had been searched, she had overseen it, and the bed had been checked, under the mattress, everywhere that he could possibly hide something. The carpet was old, but clean, she smiled to herself, this was a careful man, somebody who was used to looking after himself and who like to live in a clean, tidy space. She rested her hand on the door handle, leaning back against the wall. Where would she hide something, if she had something to hide? She pulled the door towards her, and checked the pockets of the dressing gown that hung there, taking it off the peg and checking the seam and hem. Nothing. Sighing, she put her finger through the tag in the collar to hang it up again, and then she stood still. It was so tiny, nobody had noticed it. A piece of cotton, running from the hook to the top of the door. Laying the dressing gown down again, she fetched a chair from the kitchen, and climbed up.

The door was hollow. A flat door with no beading or panels, just flat painted wood, and the cotton ran from the hook to the top of the door. Carefully, she ran her finger under the cotton, and eased the thicker twine which hung inside the door. Out came a small bag, made of thin nylon. She eased it out, fearful that it might drop back, and snap the cotton.

Once the bag was in her hand, she climbed down from the chair. She carried the bag back to the kitchen, and pulled on a pair of gloves, shaking out an evidence bag. She unzipped the bag, and pulled out the contents.

There were photos, of a little girl, a halo of blonde hair caught in the sunlight, feeding the ducks in a park. Her face was a study of concentration. The second one was the same child with a woman. Pretty woman, happy with the child, playing, laughing at something together. Behind the photos were two envelopes. One contained a will, which was signed and dated in 2015. Gemma skimmed through it, everything was left to Julia. The other envelope had two letters in it. One was to Julia, and one was not in English.

She sat at the table and read the letter from a man to his daughter, who he clearly loved very dearly, but had never met properly. She sniffed back her tears, wishing in some small mean part of her soul that her Father had ever expressed his love for her in the same way, or at all. Shaking her head, she pushed the photos and documents into the evidence bag. She checked the other doors, but they had no cotton holding surprises.

Gemma carried her find back to the car. It made no difference to the case, except that she could see him as a person, with flaws, of course, but not a complete monster. Whatever he had done, and it seemed he had done a great deal, he had loved his daughter. She leaned her head back on the seat. Was she liking him more, because he was so different from the cold hardness of her own father? Maybe, but what other yardstick had she, when comparing Fathers generally?

27.

"I can start work today. I feel fine. I've checked the website, and it says I should be up to light work today, so I'd like to start again, not feel useless, please Jamie." She handed around the cups of tea to the crew.

"OK, but maybe just for the morning, let's take it one step at a time? Take a break if you need one, and nothing too heavy." He nodded at Joe, who nodded back.

"Right, let's have a tea break then." Joe took a sip and they all laughed.

The pipes for the plumbing and central heating had arrived, and the plumbers were already busy. The joists were being fitted to hold the floors and ceilings, and the wood had to be carried inside, to keep it dry and keep the carpenters busy. All morning she lifted and listened to the drills and power planes. By lunchtime she was ready for a break and a sandwich, and Mick was pleased to have some time with her too. The staircase arrived shortly after, in sections, ready to be fitted, just as soon as they had a floor to be reached. Jamie had been right, she was tired. She made her excuses and got out of the way.

Her phone rang. Lou wanted to know what had happened between her and Amanda. "She was a snivelling mess. I've never seen her cry before. What happened?"

"I wasn't going to tell anyone, it was just such a shock seeing her. Lou, if I tell you, you can't tell other people, OK?"

"Of course, I wouldn't."

"Mike was having an affair with Amanda. That's why he left. They were going to live in Tintagel. I only found out a couple of days ago. Mike died, probably on the way to meet her. They found his body, Lou."

"What? Amanda was sleeping with your Mike?" Lou took a breath. "I don't believe it. I mean I do, but I can't take it in."

"I know, I'm still trying to get my head round it."

"God, he really was a shit, wasn't he?"

"Yes." Julia laughed. "Maybe I should thank her, she did me a favour."

"I wouldn't go that far." They were both laughing now.

"No, perhaps you're right." She shrugged in a breath. "Thanks Lou. I should have told you first, then I could have avoided a slanging match with slag pants."

"Slag pants? Is that what we're calling her?"

"Until I come up with something more ingenious." They laughed some more, and Lou promised to come over to see how far the house had come.

Jamie was waving to her when she hung up. She walked over to the site, and he called her inside.

"Look. You have a floor." She lifted her eyes, and sure enough, there was a floor upstairs, she had thought it would take longer, but once the joists were in, laying the floor had been fast. She climbed the ladder and stood on her new floor. The view from what would be her bedroom window was every bit as fabulous as she had hoped it would be. It felt safe and yet, as though she was floating in mid-air.

"Oh wow. Thank you so much. This is everything I hoped it would be."

Jamie stood and looked out with her. "This is going to be an amazing space. The stairs will be in tomorrow, and the electricians should be out by the end of the week. Plumbers shortly after, then plasterers. We're getting there. You'll be in before the end of the summer."

"Thank you, Jamie. I know you've worked really hard on this. I really appreciate it." She smiled across at him.

"None of my business, but I'm glad to see you happy with my mate Ben. He's been lonely since, well for the longest time, couldn't be with a nicer girl." He blushed around his ears.

"That's sweet Jamie. Hang on, been lonely since, what happened?" She turned away from the view.

"He'll tell you about it, when he's ready. It's not for me to say." Jamie found something on the floor very interesting.

"Something happened?"

"Don't push me, I shouldn't have said anything."

"OK. Is it something I should ask Ben about?"

"No. He'll tell you if you give him time."

"OK." She took a breath, trying to work out what it meant. "Thanks, Jamie."

She watched the vans and trucks out of the drive. Mick loped across the grass towards to her, he had found a ball and chased wildly when she threw it for him.

When Ben drove in, she was thinking about stopping, the dog was panting, but loving it. He climbed out of the car and came to wrap his arms around her.

"Hello you." He kissed her gently, his lips grazing hers softly.

"Hi yourself. How was your day?"

"Busy, lots of cats." He lifted his arm to show the scratches, laughing.

"I have a floor." She told him. "Come and see. I think Jamie took the ladders down, so I couldn't go back up there on my own, but you can see there's an upstairs, just no stairs."

"Oh wow. The view must be amazing." He looked up at the new floor.

"It's great. Jamie's done a really good job. He's been great." She smiled across at him.

"Did you work today?"

"Only this morning. Just carrying in the joists and stuff, with Joe. I stopped at lunchtime. Taking it gently." She nodded at his firm expression. "I'm being sensible, don't worry."

"I know, sorry. I just, it freaked me out a bit when you disappeared. I felt like, I suppose, out of control." He turned away from her and looked out at the view.

"It's OK, it must have been scary. I was frightened too, for a bit. I came home though." She stood behind him and leaned her head against his back, her arms around him.

"I was just worried, that's all." He turned towards her and smiled. They walked across the grass to the shed, and spent the evening together, eating, chatting, laughing, walking the dog, and finally curling up together, under her quilt as the night settled around them.

"I'm surprised how quickly the house is coming together." He shifted his weight, so he could see her face.

"I know, I wanted, only to be in there before the cold weather comes, but I think it will be faster than that."

"Julia. I have something I should tell you. I keep on trying to, but then the moment is gone, and I chicken out. I'm rubbish at this stuff." She turned her head on the pillow so she could look him in the eye, and waited. "At school, I was involved with a girl. Diana. She was lovely, you would have liked her. We were madly in love, like teenagers are. No reservations, no holding back, no being careful." He wiped a hand across his forehead. "As it turned out, that was a step too far. Diana got pregnant, and when we found out, we were, understandably, terrified. We decided to get married. We planned it all, she could come with me to Uni, I had a place at Bristol, and we'd have the baby and it would be alright. We went to see the doctor and we talked to my parents, they said they would help us. They weren't happy but they could see we were trying to be sensible about it. Then we went to see her Dad. Looking back, we were too full of it, too excited to see that his reaction wouldn't be as reasonable. I didn't see it coming. He smacked me across the head, and I was out cold. When I woke up, they were both gone. My head was ringing. I got out of the house, and went looking for them. I walked for three hours. I couldn't find them. I went home and my parents phoned the police. They looked everywhere, but she was gone. A week later, they found them, he'd killed her, then himself."

"Oh Ben, I'm so sorry, that must have been devastating for you." She stroked her hand across his arm.

"No, well, yes, but that's not why I'm telling you." He took a deep breath. "When Florian took you. I saw him grab you and throw you in the van. I ran and chased, and drove like a maniac, but I couldn't find you. It brought back that feeling, that helpless, dreadful hole in my head, where I can't think about what happens next, and I can't hear because everything is too loud to concentrate. The panic that floods everything and swamps my brain. All of that. Again. I'm a mess." A single tear tipped down his cheek. He didn't brush it away.

"I'm so sorry, that you felt like that at all, and that I made you feel like that again." She kissed the tear away, her hands soft on his face.

He wrapped his arms around her, pulling her closer, gripping her tightly to him, his face buried in her hair.

28.

"Anya?" She caught her breath.

"Hello. Hello. How are you feeling?"

"I am so much better. Because of you. You made me better, and you made me happy. First time in too many years." She took a breath. "Florian tells me you made a deal before you leave."

"Yes."

"He says you think I only want to know you because I am sick. Not because you are my daughter. Is this true?"

"I hoped it wasn't, but I don't know you well enough to know for sure."

"I want to come and see you. When the doctor says it is safe. Florian will bring me."

"OK."

"It makes me sad, that you don't trust. I understand why, but it makes me sad. I want to talk to you, so we can learn more and get to know each other. Then maybe you can trust a little more?"

"I'd like that. Come when you are well enough, and we'll spend some time together." Julia's face split with a smile.

"Can you tell me something in the meantime?"

"Yes."

"My husband. Florian says he is missing. Do you know what happened?" Julia could hear the quake in her mother's voice.

"I don't know. I know that Florian said he met him. I did meet him, but I didn't know he was my father. He used to sit having coffee at the beach in the mornings. He'd say hello, or good morning. I wish I'd known he was my father, that he'd told me. I know that the Police found my ex-boyfriend's body on his land." She took a breath. "I think that they believe he was killed by my father."

"Your Father was a criminal, a violent man. He was also funny, and generous and kind. He was handsome, when we were young. He would laugh and snatch me up in his arms and swing me through the air. He was strong. I loved him with all my heart. When he left to work in England, I knew there would be other women, there always had been. When he stayed away, in a way I wasn't surprised. I wasn't enough for him. When he left, I was already pregnant with you, so you were my baby, just you and me. Florian remembered him, but you were all mine, until they took you." Her voice cracked.

"I'm sorry. Please don't cry. Look, I have to tell you something, I don't know if I got it wrong, but I think the Police want to talk to Florian about our father's disappearance. Maybe just to check what happened when he did see him." Julia leaned against the step, and felt Mick lean against her leg.

"Do you think.... What are you saying?"

"I don't know anything more than what I said. The Police are looking into the whole thing, which would suggest that they think there was someone else involved. If Florian was the last person who saw him, he might be able to help with their investigation. Maybe he should know that they want to talk to him, then he can decide what to do?" Julia closed her eyes. What was she doing? Was she interfering too much? Not enough? This was all new to her, and she had no point of reference. Was she warning her brother, did she really believe he needed warning?

"Good idea, I'll speak to him and see what he thinks is the best thing to do." She drew a breath. "You're a good girl Anya, a good sister. I'll call you again soon."

Julia held the phone to her chest. A breath shuddered in and out. She watched her fingers grip each other and jumped when it rang.

"Julia? Hi It's Gemma." Sweat prickled the skin between Julia's shoulder blades.

"Hi, Gemma. How are you?" She pushed her hand out until it hit the hard wood of the door frame. Solid and warm from the sunshine.

"You OK?"

"Yes, fine, thanks."

"Just checking you're OK. Did you hear from your brother at all? I need to straighten out a few things with him."

"No, I haven't heard from him. Sorry."

"Not your fault. Let me know if you hear anything?"

"Yes of course."

She sat down holding the phone tightly, and closed her eyes. Her fingers stretched straight, and hit redial, before she could think about it.

"Julia?"

"Gemma. Sorry. I lied." She wiped her face with the back of her hand. "Not exactly, but I did. I spoke to my mother, not my brother. I told her that you wanted to speak to him. I don't know about this stuff, I have only just started having a brother. I don't know if I wanted to warn him or get him back here. I'm sorry."

"Don't be. It's OK. I sort of thought you would." Gemma cleared her throat. "I don't know if it helps. But I would expect a normal family member to behave exactly as you have. I expected the same from you. I have contacts in other forces and they are looking for Florian. At some point, he will turn up, and when that happens, I will talk to him. I'll be in a line, waiting, there are other, higher=ranking investigations which will take precedence. I can also tell you, that your father was a big name in the criminal world, until he took a step back a few years ago. He was a dangerous man who lived a very complicated life. His son is a lot like him." Gemma took a breath. "You are not being unreasonable in finding this hard to deal with, or confusing. It's OK. All I'm asking is that you keep me in the loop as much as you can."

"OK." Her voice was small, and her face was wet.

"Good enough. Take some time. I'll call you in a few days." Gemma hung up.

Julia sat alone, in the peace of her shed, and Mick sat close by.

29.

Ben waited on the beach. He could see Mick's head lifted above the water, bobbing up and down as he swam towards the shore, then circled back to Julia. He sat on the warm sand and watched them play. They swam towards him, side by side, and he met them at the surf. He felt foolish and heroic and strangely sexy, and all of those things were fine with him. He would have cared, a few weeks ago, if people thought he was stupid or weak or laughable, but today he would take all of that, to feel like he did at that moment, watching this woman drag her legs through the surf towards him, in a wet suit and surrounded by a barking happy dog. The sun sparkled on the water, his eyes narrowed against the light, and he felt his face stretch wider into a smile that felt more real and more his own than he could remember feeling. Mick shook his fur dry sending water spraying over them both. He laughed and watched Julia's face crease into a smile.

A voice carried across the sand towards them. The smile fell off Julia's face and she stepped back and reached down to rest her hand on Mick's head.

"Julia. Please Julia, please talk to me."

"Amanda, I'm not really up for that today."

"I want to apologise."

"You have, and I'm glad you have, but you can't imagine that we're going to be friends again."

"I had. I imagined that we were good enough friends to get

through this." Amanda's voice hardened.

"Hang on, are you actually saying that you're getting angry with me about this?" Julia chewed her lip. "You've got a nerve. How dare you? After what you did, you think you can demand that I be your friend again. Do you know what Amanda? Don't talk to me, don't come near me again. I don't want to be your friend. I don't want to be anything to you, or anywhere you are. I've learned some uncomfortable things about where I come from over the last few weeks, and a lot of them I don't like, but I have come to understand a little about loyalty and what it means. My Father over reacted to your affair with Mike, but at least he reacted. I won't dishonour that history by sweeping your behaviour under the carpet and accepting you back into my life." She took a breath and for a moment he thought she would say more, but she walked away, Mick trotting at her heels to keep up across the sand. He followed her, and caught up with her as she stripped the wet suit off her shoulders. Her face was red and tears spilled from her eyes.

"Julia. Come on. Let's go home." Gently he wrapped his arms around her. She was shaking.

"Do you know what? I have always had a temper. Mum used to say the person who loses their temper loses the argument, and I learned to control it, but I have his blood in my veins, my father, the killer, a gangster. I think my brother is the same. Just then, I understood them, I could have hit her and kept on hitting. The strange thing is that I'm over Mike, it's not about that. It was the betrayal, the fact that she carried on pretending all these years, and laughing at me behind my back." Tears flowed unchecked as she sat in the car, her arms around Mick. He rested his hand on her shoulder, the flesh cold and damp under his fingers. "I need to find a different beach to swim at." Her voice was cold.

He drove her home and watched her turn back into herself a little more while they toured the site. She was excited and looking forward to the house. He held her hand as they climbed the hill together and slumped next to her on the grass.

"You can say no if you like, but my Mum has asked if you'd like to meet her, well the whole lot of them, for Sunday lunch. She does cook a fantastic roast dinner, but it does mean being with my family, Mum, Dad, three sisters, two brothers in law, two nieces and two nephews. Do you fancy it?" He watched her think about it.

"Meet the parents?" She raised an eyebrow. "What are they like?"

"Like most people, they're mostly nice, and a bit grumpy sometimes. My Mum worries a lot, my Dad gets grumpy and stomps off down the garden. My sisters are OK most of the time, they fight, but mostly between themselves. My nieces are OK, but very pink. My nephews are amazing, so much fun." He shrugged.

"That sounds refreshingly normal. Yes please, I'd love to meet them." She smiled and reached an arm across to touch him. "Sorry about earlier."

"Don't be. She's a cow." He giggled, and so did she.

30.

His eyes opened a crack. He could see it was light outside. He moved, slowly, carefully taking his legs sideways off the bed. The door was locked, he tried it anyway. The window was nailed shut and he knew the shutters were noisy when he moved them yesterday, or was it the day before, time was a little hazy.

He sat slowly on the bed, and closed his eyes. He had to sort through the jumble in his head, but it was so hard to find where to start. He had done some things in his life. He knew that. His Father had always said he was evil, he'd taken him to church, asked the priest to help, beaten him and locked him up, none of it had changed him. If anything, he just got better at taking the beatings, and at giving them too. If you took a beating, you knew what hurt most. He grew bigger and stronger, until he could get away from his Father and his blundering stupidity. He had walked out of the house one morning and not gone back, walked away from the village and found himself a few days later in the town, and six months later in a bigger town. He had learned his lessons well, his Father had taught him that people feared him, and he used his hard-won skills to make money, he had thought himself rich back then. His body was strong and hard, and his fists were ready. He was a good thief, he could have carried on stealing, if he had avoided meeting Jorge, who offered him more money than he had dreamed possible. Selling little packets of powder was so much easier than off loading jewellery or breaking into houses, where there might be dogs. His customers paid on time, and if they were late, he dealt with it. Jorge showed him how to run a team, showed him how to run the business, where to collect the bigger packets of powder. He had been glad to learn, and soon, Jorge was in his way, and then he was gone.

He met her the night after he made his own deal with the suppliers. He was in charge now, and they had talked about him going abroad, taking parcels for them, if everything worked out. She was pretty, and clean looking, not the sort of girl he usually went for. He usually liked girls who wore dresses that clung to them and short skirts. She was quiet, and when he took her home, and she stepped back when he tried to kiss her, he was strangely delighted.

A few months later they went to church and a fat priest with bad breath murmured his way through a wedding service. She was nervous and somehow that made him feel stronger, and braver. He was young, and looking back now, he realized how stupid. She loved him, and he took her for granted. He thought he was being a man. The laugh that bubbled through him sounded hollow inside. He had carried on as before, working, and drinking. His wife had dinner on the table every night for him, and was excited when he got home in time to eat it, and as time went on, stopped expecting him to come home. She still made dinner, and accepted that most nights the neighbour's dog ate it. When she found out that she was pregnant, she was worried to tell him. He had watched her flitting about, nervous and anxious stumbling over her words. He had told her he was happy and smiled when she sank into a chair with relief. The night Florian was born, he had been miles away collecting on a debt. By the time he got back, the baby had arrived, and was wrapped in a blue blanket. His wife was bathed and clean, her hair brushed back and her face flushed.

He had told himself over the years, that he had built the business to give them a better life, then he changed the story, imagined they would be safer if he stayed away. Too late, he realized his mistakes, after he watched Janice take his daughter, and give her the love he couldn't. He took stock, accepted who and what he was and gave his energy to what he was good at.

All he had achieved, everything he had done, had brought him to this thin mattress on a creaking bed frame in this dank hapless room, and a visit every day from his landlord.

Now that he was old, and he could look back, with experience and understanding, he had nothing to do but think, and all the time he could need to do it.

His mouth was dry and his tongue seemed too big for his mouth. He checked his fingertips, they felt numb as he rubbed them along his forearm, and he waited.

31.

Florian rolled over, his head hurt and his eyes were gritty. His phone showed seven missed calls, one from the girl he was supposed to meet the night before, Laura was his off and on girlfriend, he knew he should be better, kinder to her, but there were too many other things to think about. Two of the calls were definitely work and the others from his mother. He closed his eyes again and tried not to think about the thumping in his head. He knew what his mother wanted, she had rung him every day since she has spoken to Julia, worried that the police wanted to talk to him, and wanting him to take her to Cornwall. He was unsurprised by the first and, at the moment, unable to make her happy on the second, so he had been ignoring her for the last few days in the hope that she would leave him alone. He had another issue he needed to address and today was perhaps the right time.

He felt better for a shower and a coffee, and the painkillers were starting to work, so he drove the mile and a half from his flat to the run-down street, where he needed to ask some questions. Inside, the smell of damp and dirt made his nostrils twitch. The man he had left in charge showed him up to a small bedroom and unlocked the door.

"Hello." He walked in, keeping his tone and his expression neutral. The first word he had spoken to this man in over twenty years.

"Florian." It was a statement, not a question.

"You know me then? You recognize me?"

"You look like me, and a little like your mother." He shrugged. "Who else would be interested in me?"

"As far as I can work out, a lot of people are interested in you. The friends you left in London, the friends you left in Albania, your Wife, your daughter, the Police. Me." No reply came. "I met her, you know, your perfect clean daughter. She didn't know you were her father, or who her family are. She believed Janice was her only family. She was happy though, that you bought her the house, and a necklace." He shrugged. "I want to know why you left our mother, and why you never came looking for us. Why you left us to rot, to stay with Uncles and Aunts, dependant on them."

The old man took a breath, long and deep. He raised his head to his son, and watched his own eyes look back.

"I heard about you, too. I heard you made a name for yourself in Manchester, that you were a force to be reckoned with. You were brave, coming over here, so young. I didn't want them to bring her, you must have known that. I wanted them to bring you. I didn't know your Mum was pregnant when I left. I wanted my son. I was young and stupid, and I made mistakes. I was concentrating on building a business here. I thought I would help you both, but as time went on, I always found other things I needed to do." He shook his head, as if he couldn't believe his stupidity himself.

"We were hungry, a lot of the time, when I was a child, and cold. I didn't care, I had never known anything else, but my mother suffered, she still loves you, even now. She wants all of us to be a family together, her daughter, her husband." He huffed a laugh. "The woman is not reasonable."

"I know. It's my fault, I should never have married her so fast. All she wanted was a family, a safe settled life. The only thing I couldn't give her. I loved her once, though. She was good and kind and I felt better when I was with her, but it was no life for me. I was grateful when I walked away." The silence stretched.

Being sorry was no excuse for bad behaviour, but it was true. "What did you bring me here for?"

"I don't know." Florian closed his eyes. "I wanted to kill you, I wanted to beat you with my fists until you were dead, but I wanted to talk to you more."

"So. Talk."

"Now that you're here, I don't have anything to say." Florian leaned against the door frame, his body sagging under the weight of his thoughts.

"Do you remember I bought you a little truck? It was red I think, on my last visit home. You liked it, you rolled it all over the house."

"It was blue." His voice was flat.

"You liked it though? Do you remember liking it?"

"I do. I used to keep it in my coat pocket, like a good luck charm. My uncle took it from me and gave it to my cousin. He didn't even like it, he just kept it because I wanted it. Last thing I did before I left Albania was to punch that smug fuck in the face." He laughed.

"You grew up in a hard place. Perhaps you'll be angry enough to kill me. Perhaps we can work together, I don't know. I don't understand why you brought me here. If you wanted to kill me, you could have done it when you came to my place. I have had time to think, to regret, how I have lived. I am old, I have made more mistakes than you can imagine, but I have also done some good things. If you would agree, I would like to see your mother, before it's time for me to go. I want to apologise, make my peace." He shrugged.

"Don't." Florian pushed himself from the door frame and walked away. It was too much.

He sat in the car, waiting for his head to clear. His phone rang, and called him to work, and so he had no time to think, blocking out the problems with his family, and putting his energy into what he needed to do.

Late in the evening, when he was heading home, he had time to think again, and found that he had driven back to the house. His Father was sitting on the bed.

"What do you mean, we could work together?"

"I meant, I know your business, I was in the same line of work. Perhaps I could help you, or perhaps we could do something different together. Florian, neither of us went to a proper school, but we are smart, otherwise we wouldn't have made money, or a life here. I am old now, I got out, because I could see that there was money to be made which was easier to get to. I might be able to help you there too. I also meant that we could work together to see if we can make your mother happy again. I owe her that." His head was low, his chin almost resting on his chest. He made no move to stand or to meet Florian's eye.

32.

The house smelled like a hospital, it was so highly bleached and scrubbed. She had always worried about dirt, and now, knowing that she was unwell, made her more careful than ever. Florian had bought her presents, over the years, little ornaments, made of china and glass, which she washed and dusted to keep them looking as new as the first day she had received them. Each one stood in place, evidence and a reminder of what a good son she had. How caring, and loving she had brought him up to be. She had heard rumours, of course, but she chose to ignore those. He had risen fast in the building trade, earned good money, and it made people jealous. She had spent a lifetime feeling envious of other people, families, who were together, who nobody had ripped apart, who had enough money, who could give their children everything they needed. That hard, bitter part of her was hidden, wrapped in the belief that she had somehow contributed to her own pain. She had known what he was, she had known about his business, and his reputation. She had even known about the other women. She had believed, made herself believe that they were unimportant, that he came home to her, and that she was the one he loved, the one who gave him a son, and kept everything running at home. She let him run his business, she stepped back, she was the perfect, uncomplaining, supportive wife. Prepared to do what it took, and left with nothing, not even her daughter. Not even her pride. Her sisters had been delighted to see her fall. To have her depend on them, to feel superior. She had bitten her tongue, been subservient, given them the gift of her pride in return for a home and food for her son. She had cleaned their houses, cooked the dinners, and swallowed the resentment she had felt along with the vegetables and chicken she stewed.

The day Florian had first come home with cash in his pockets, the hairs at the base of her skull had lifted away from her skin, the contractions which twisted and squeezed her gut were familiar and almost comforting. Fear and guilt were old friends, she knew how to deal with them. She watched her son, not a child anymore, not fully grown yet, she could see he would fill out, and be stronger, but he already had the look in his eyes, the one she had seen in his father's, the one which told her he would do whatever it took to get what he wanted. He showed her the money he had earned, and the ticket he had bought, and promised to send one for her. She kissed him goodbye, holding his face in her hands, her lips lingering on his cheeks. Later, she buried her smiles at the broken nose spread across her brother in law's face, and the split lip swelling on her nephew's mouth, which made it hard to eat his dinner.

Seven months later, she received a ticket through the post and left without much fuss. Her son stood waiting at the airport, and she was relieved, not happy, but some of the fear and pain of her life lifted away from her. She had moved into her home that day, Florian paid the rent, the bills, and gave her money to spend. He came to dinner once a week, and brought her gifts, or flowers. He remembered her birthday, and enjoyed her dinner. She wanted, more than anything she had ever dreamed of, to have her daughter back, to make them a family, and feel like a mother again. Perhaps, one day, a grandmother. The idea made her smile.

She knew, maybe better than people thought she did, about her son. He was like his father, he lived too fast, drank too much, dated women she would not have approved of if she had met them. She looked the other way and saw nothing of his faults. She saw the good, kind, generous son who had listened to her stories with wide eyes and snuggled his body against hers, his warm little shape as he slept the only comfort in that bleak time. They had become a team, working together to get through the difficulties that life without his father brought, and despite his faults, and she knew them as well as she knew her own, she trusted him, and she knew he trusted her. That was what they had, they knew how hard life could be, and they knew that they were stronger together, and that strength was the way to make life better.

She still felt tired too quickly and slept fitfully. She could not have cared less. Her dream was coming true. She had sat in a bed in the hospital and he had brought the only person she had wanted to see. She had held the hands she had spent her nights wishing for, and seen the face she had dreamed of since her baby was pulled from her arms and taken away. She had wiped the tears that her daughter had cried and wrapped her arms around the woman her baby had become, and nothing in the world could have been better or could have given her back the pieces that had been missing for so long. No matter what Florian did, however many laws he broke, she knew he had not broken faith with her. He had saved her life and given her something to spend that life living for.

The net curtain hung bright and white in the sunlight. She pushed it back and watched from the window, recognizing her neighbours and the children who played in the street. Life was slow and she found that watching the lives she could see from her window made the time pass happily. She had learned to wave and nod her greetings, but had been worried to take a further step, and meet her neighbours. Her lack of confidence in her ability to speak the language clearly enough, and to understand what people said to her held her inside and kept her door closed.

Today, though, would bring her son, her joy and her life would arrive within the hour, and dinner was ready. She sat, her feet tucked around each other, her slippers warm on her feet, waiting to see his car pull up. It was always the moment that she loved, when he climbed out of the car, and looked up to her window, his face creasing into a smile when he saw her waiting for him.

"Mama." He let himself into the hallway.

"Florian. My son. My love." Her hand rested gently against his face, and she felt his arms wrap around her. "Come, dinner is ready." She spooned his plate full and sat nibbling the edges of hers. He ate and each mouthful filled a space in her as much as in his belly.

"I have been chatting with my father." He kept his eyes on his plate.

"Your Papa? What does he say?"

"He says he wants to talk to you, to apologise, for what he did, how he treated you. Would you like to see him?" He looked carefully at her face. "Up to you. It's not up to him."

She stood up from the table, and went to the counter. She had made a cake for him. She cut a slice, while she thought. He was alive. He wanted to see her. Her chest squeezed with the tears that she had kept there for so many years. Was it enough that he had asked? Maybe she really could say no. The cake oozed with icing and syrup. She slid it across the table to him.

"What does he look like? Does he look old?" She pushed a fork to him.

"He looks older. He is carrying a little more weight than I remember and his hair is grey. You've aged better. You're still beautiful Mama." He forked the cake into his mouth. "This is good. You don't have to decide today. You can call me when you decide." His eyebrows lifted.

"There's nothing to decide. I'll see him. I want to." She covered his hand with hers.

"OK. Do you want me to bring him here? Or somewhere else?"

"Here. My house. My ground." She nodded, and cut herself a small slice of the cake. He was right, it was good.

33.

She watched the car pull up, and the two men she loved climb out. Florian was right, he was a little wider around the middle, and his hair which had been blonde as a young man had faded with grey. Florian watched him, he pointed to the door of the house, and nodded at something his father said. Together they walked to the door, and she pulled herself up straight, her head held high, knowing that she only had seconds before he would be in her living room. She wondered what he would make of her. Perhaps he would think she had become an old lady, and maybe he would be right.

"Mama." Florian's voice was loud, in the quiet of her house.

"Florian, my love." She walked into the living room. Her son stood between them, careful and edgy.

"Katya. It's been a long time." His face was lined, and his skin was brown from the sun. His shoulders were less square than they had been last time she saw him. His eyes were the same. He looked at her the same way he had when they were young.

"Alexi? I was unsure if that was a good idea. It has been too long. I thought you were dead."

"I'm sorry Katya, truly sorry. I was too young and too selfish to be married. I didn't behave well."

"You stole my baby." Her voice was low. Her eyes were wet and she blinked to clear the tears.

"I am sorry for that too. I have done some terrible things in my life. I have killed people, I have sold drugs, and I have been unkind and vicious, but of all the things I regret, taking the baby was the worst. I think you have met her though, which I haven't. I have seen her, but I didn't tell her who I was, I didn't want to mess up her life again." His eyes studied the carpet between his feet.

"Look at me. Lex." His eyes snapped up to meet hers.

"That's a name I haven't been called for a long time. I've missed that Kat. I miss who I was when you used to call me Lex. I know it was a long time ago, and too much has happened, but thank you for letting me apologise." His smile spread a little wider, and his eyes crinkled at the sides.

"Do you still take your coffee the same way?" She caught his smile, and nodded, getting up she walked to the kitchen and brought back coffee and her home-made cake. He tasted it and nodded, licking his fingers.

"This is wonderful. Can I say something else?" She nodded. "Our children are beautiful, that's down to both of us. But Florian is smart, and he's determined, that's all you. I gave you no help, and no hope, but you did a good job. Florian is a credit to you." She smiled, accepting his compliment.

"I remember you, I recall how you work. You check out the most important thing to a person, and you praise them for that, in your humility, or you hurt them through that, use it to hurt them. I have had time to think through every conversation we ever had, every time you pushed me to accept your bad behaviour. You didn't have to push, you didn't have to manipulate, I loved you, I would have done what was needed to keep you safe, to keep our family safe, without you having to make me." She lifted her cake, then thought again and put it on her plate. "You are right, though. Florian is a wonderful son. It's not my work alone, he worked hard, as a child, he took responsibility for himself when I was too weakened by my depression to function. He looked after me, he took all the bullying that came from his Uncles and his cousins. His own strength made him who he is."

"Mama!" Florian shook his head. "Stop now, you did your best. The depression wasn't so bad."

"See how he protects you?" He nodded at his son. "I am the bad guy here. I know that. That's why I had to say sorry before its too late."

"Why will it be too late? Are you ill?" Her eyebrows pushed together.

"No." He held his hands out in front of him. "It's an expression, and we're all getting older. I have not lived a clean and healthy life, I've drunk too much, and eaten far too much red meat." He looked down at his plate. "Not enough cake like this, though."

"Would you like to meet Anya?" She asked him, and watched his confusion. "Julia. Would you like to meet Julia?"

"Yes. Please. Was that what you called her? Anya? It's pretty." He turned to his son. "Did your Mama tell you that she chose your name?"

"No." Florian shrugged his shoulders.

"I was away from home when you were born, you were early, by a week. I got home, and there you were, red in the face from screaming, and your Mama sitting up in bed, with her hair all brushed the wrong way. She said, this is your son, his name is Florian. I said, don't I get a choice? She said, you give birth, you can decide what to name the baby." He laughed. "You were the tiniest person I ever saw, and so loud. I watched you screaming and waving your arms, until your Mama picked you up, and then you calmed right down, and I felt like it would be alright. The terror that had filled me when I first saw you, just drifted away. It came back, obviously, but only for twenty or so hours of the day." He smiled. The memories were good ones.

"I remember that. You timed it perfectly, getting home an hour after everything was over. He was beautiful then, and he still is." It was a statement of fact.

"There were no mobile phones in those days, I had no way to know. What happened with Anya? Were you with your sisters?" He leaned forward towards her.

"Yes, both of them were there. Anya was quick to arrive." A tear fell slowly down her face. "I thought I had never been so lonely as that night, after she was born, and they left, and I sat with her, and wondered how long we would have to wait to see her father. I walked around that house, saw Florian asleep, saw the baby sleep, and I felt so sorry for myself. I was a spoiled child, and inside out with hormones doing their worst. A few years later I wished for that night so many times. I wished I had taken my two beautiful children and run away, hidden somewhere that we all would have been safe. Where your thugs couldn't have found us, but I didn't, I sat there like a fool, and waited for my husband to come home and see what a wonderful surprise was waiting for him." She wiped her finger slowly under her eye. "I have cried too many tears over the years since Anya was born, and missed too much. I want to look forward to what comes next, to getting to know the woman she became, under someone else's care. Without me." She turned her tea cup while she focused her thoughts. "All I want, is for all of us, all of our family to be together, to try to mend the damage that has been done, and send our two children forward without the baggage they are carrying at the moment." She met his gaze, and waited in silence.

"That sounds like a good way to go. I would like to get to know both of our children if they both want that, and anything,

173

anything that makes even a very small dent in the way I behaved." He nodded, and turned to his son. "Florian, what do you think?"

"I don't know what to think, except that my mother is more generous than you deserve. I'll phone my sister and ask her if she wants to come and see you both, and see what can be done." His eyes searched his father's face, but it was no more open than his own, so he made the call.

"Julia? Hi, it's Florian. Yes, everything is fine. I have something to ask you. Our parents are sitting in the same room for the first time since before you were born, and they have asked me to phone you, to see if you would like to come up to visit and spend some time getting to know them both. What do you think?" He turned away from his parent's watchful eyes. "OK, I understand, that's fine. Will you phone me back? On this number? Thanks Julia. Bye." He turned back to see both of them on the edge of their seats. "She would like to see you both, and she will come, but she has to get someone to look after her dog, and sort out a few things there. She'll call me back when she has made the arrangements." He sat back down and looked at them both. "Are you sure about this? Remember, she does not know either of you, and she has had a very different life from us."

"I am sure. I want to try. Whether or not your Papa stays around, I want to know my daughter." He turned to his Father who nodded in agreement.

34.

July 2018

The train was only a little late, and the train station was busy. She pulled her suitcase behind her along the platform and through the gate. People were moving in every direction. She stood still, and checked the crowd for a face she knew.

"Anya? My Anya." Her Mother pushed through the people between them, rushing to take her daughter's face in her hands. "Oh, my girl, you came." She wrapped a hug around Julia which was fierce and strong, and took her by surprise.

"Hello. How are you feeling? You look well." Julia hugged her mother. It was a strange feeling, but was the reason, after all, for her visit, to learn more about her family and to get to know them.

"Come. Florian and your Papa are in the car." She held onto Julia's hand and pulled her through the station, chatting fast and wearing a huge smile, turning to check that Julia was smiling back at her. She stopped just short of the entrance, and turned again to Julia, taking her face in her hands and kissing her cheeks. "Thank you for coming." She didn't wait for a reply but bustled off again, and into the waiting car.

"Hello Julia." Florian was in the driving seat, and he turned to look at his sister. "This is our father."

The man in the passenger seat turned to see her. She recognised him from the beach. "No swimming today?" His face crinkled.

"No, not today. I have a message for you though." She pulled her phone out of her pocket, and opened a video she had taken the day before. Mick chased a ball across the grass and returned with it in his mouth, looking healthy and happy. "Mick says to tell you hello."

"You have my dog?" His eyes almost disappeared beneath his furrowed brows.

"He turned up at my house, tired and hungry, and he moved in. Ben said he knew you, and recognised the dog, he checked the chip and said he was definitely your dog, but nobody knew where you had gone, so he stayed with me. He's a lovely dog." She chewed her lip. "I didn't recognize him from the beach. I should have, but he was so dirty and thin."

"I'm so glad you have him, he must have come to you, to be with family. How wonderful." He laughed and it was a deep rumble from his chest.

They chatted and it occurred to Julia that they were strangers, as closely as they might be linked by genetics, they still were strangers and the four of them talked about nothing and circled each other carefully, not wanting to give offence, or to jump in too fast. At her mother's house there was enough food for ten, and clearly, she had been working hard to get everything ready. Finally, they sat down in the uncomfortable sofas to talk.

"Can I ask some questions?" Julia looked around the room and received nods. "Tell me about why I was brought to England, and why you let Janice take me away from you?" Her Father nodded again.

"I was young, and selfish, I was having a good time in England, living an expensive life, but I wanted my son. I didn't want to be married, so I sent people to take my child, it was the worst thing I could have done, to my wife, but I didn't think about it." He shook his head. "When you arrived, I didn't understand, I hadn't even known Katya was pregnant. You were so pretty, but I wasn't prepared for the demands a baby makes. I had expected a little boy who talked and understood. Janice was my girlfriend at the time, she had been working for me in a restaurant I owned, but we had got together, she was smart, and funny, and a little more serious that I liked, she was getting too involved." He took a breath, his thumb rubbing over his fingers. "When you turned up, she took you over, and you loved her. Little by little, you became more hers than mine. She left, and took you with her one morning, early. I found out where she was and I watched, part of me wanted to kick the door in and take you back, but the more honest part of me knew I had no way to care for you, and she did. I left her to look after you. I watched from a distance, and made sure you were safe. I was a rubbish Father, to you and to Florian, and a worse husband. I know this now." He stopped and sat back. "We learn as we go."

"OK, I can see how that happened. Did you kill Mike Spencer?" Her eyes never left his face.

"Who?" His eyebrows lifted a little.

"My boyfriend. His body was found on your land. He left me for a friend of mine, Amanda?" He nodded. "They were going to live together in Tintagel, but he never turned up."

"I told you I watched you. When Janice died, I finished my business in London and followed you to Cornwall. I bought a place, and from a distance, I watched." He nodded. "I saw him, coming out of a pub with her, laughing, like people who had a secret. I followed them and saw them go to a hotel. It didn't take too much to work out what was happening. I booked to stay at the same hotel, and I saw them, wrapped around each other, at breakfast." His lip lifted a little as though he had tasted something sour. "They were talking about when they would live together, and when they would meet. I listened. When he had been home and packed his bags, and waited, like a coward for you to go out, I followed him. He parked his car in Tintagel, and got out, it was getting dark, and nobody was about. I hit him on the head and put him in the back of the van." His nostrils flared with remembered anger. "The disrespect, the humiliation. He woke up when we got back to my place and started banging on the sides of the van. I told him who I was. He said some terrible things, about his relationship with you. He was bragging about how much money he had made you borrow, how many years it would take you to pay it back, and meanwhile he would be spending it on his new woman. He was so arrogant, he thought he was so clever. I just hit him, lost my temper. I got my gun and I put a bullet in his head." He leaned across the gap between them. "I had killed men for less, much less. I had meant to talk to him, get him to realize he was making a mistake, running off with that woman, but I lost my temper. I dug the hole and pushed him in, with his bag, and filled the hole in." He scooped up her hand and held it in his. "I was so proud of how you managed. I wanted to help you, but how could I? I paid for some adverts for your business, put your phone number on them, to get you more customers, it was little enough. I watched that woman, pretending to be your friend, smiling when she should beg your forgiveness. I am sorry. I was just so angry that he would behave that way. Before you say I was a hypocrite, when I had done the same, and worse, I know. I have spent years thinking about it, and I am my harshest critic. He was no good. You need someone better than that." He watched her face.

"You're right. I don't agree with what you did, but I understand it. I have recently started seeing someone else, you know him, I think. Ben? The vet?" She watched a smile spread across his face.

"Much better. Decent person. If you know about the body, I suppose the Police do too?" She nodded. "OK." He nodded too.

"The Police want to talk to both of you. I haven't told them that I am coming here to see you, I haven't even told Ben where I was going, only that I was going to meet up with you. I didn't want him to have to feel like I was asking him to lie. I am here because you are my family, and I don't know who you are, and I want to." She looked at Florian. "Your turn." A smile and some understanding passed between them,

"I am here because Mama asked me to come here. I am also here because I'm angry. I have felt second best for as long as I remember. I was the one that should have been taken, the one she didn't have to miss." He scuffed his hand against the arm of the sofa. "I was there, when she couldn't get out of bed in the afternoon, when she sat in a chair and looked at nothing, for hours. I decided, one day, I guess I was twelve or a little older, that I had to get strong enough to take care of her, to find the baby that she cried for, and whatever else was needed. That's what I did. I got strong. But I'm still the second, less important one, no matter what I do, it's not enough." He closed his eyes, then turned to his Father his breath snagging on his words. "When I tracked you down, found you, part of me wanted to kill you, I wanted to hurt you. I wanted it so much, but I didn't. I brought you here, and I have resisted my instinct to kill you." He watched his Father nod. "When I found Julia, I thought, finally, I would be bringing Mama what she wanted." He rubbed his hand across his forehead. "It's not going to sort all this out, is it?"

"Florian. My love. I made you feel like that? I never thought that. I wanted my baby back, but you were my baby too. When they took her, part of me went with her, and I wasn't enough for you, but it was my fault, not yours." She reached across and held his hand. "Never your fault."

"No, it was mine." He nodded again. "I should have been honest with you. All of you."

"Ok, now we've established that all of you are happy to take the blame, can we stop, just draw a line under it and make a family, out of what we have? Honestly, I'm sorry, but I had a great childhood, I was loved and cared for, and I always slept in a warm bed and I never went hungry. My Mum, um, Janice, was a wonderful person, and I'm grateful for the time I had with her. I'm sorry it caused all of you pain, but it's the truth. Right now, I think you all need to decide if you can forgive each other, or not, and if you can, then do it, don't waste any more time." Julia sat back.

"Smart girl we made." Her Father smiled and nodded.

"We didn't though, Janice brought her up. Maybe I should be grateful to her, for taking good care of you." Her Mum rubbed a small hand across Julia's shoulders. "I never thought I would have you all here together. Dinner time." She bustled out to the kitchen.

The three of them sat together, the silence got thicker, and stretched longer between them.

"I don't know how to do this. I never thought about this part."

"I have a question." Julia sat forward, both her brother and her father looked relieved. "Why did you call your dog Mick?"

"Ah. Yes. I didn't know that Mick was a boy's name in England, in Albanian it means friend, pal, we spell it M I K." He laughed. "To begin with I used to say his name and people would laugh, I wondered what it was about."

Florian laughed. The three of them laughed together.

"What?" Katya poked her head around the door. "Tell me the joke." Florian explained, but she just shook her head and ducked out again. They laughed more.

They shared a meal, and began to feel like a family, just a little. They spent the afternoon together, and, when the evening came, Florian took their father away in his car, and Katya and Julia sat down together. Julia opened an envelope of pictures she had kept when she cleared her mother's things. "I thought you might like to see these. I got copies so you can keep these, if you wanted to."

Katya sat on the sofa, studying each picture, every detail of the little girl who grew up a little with each photo. Her fingers traced the outline of a face she had never washed, and hair that had not felt her hands through it, or brushing it, or tying ribbons in it. The woman who had cared for her baby smiled at the camera. She had a pretty face, open and laughing. She had chosen dresses for her Julia, and smoothed her hair into plaits and bunches. The little girl became a girl in school uniform and later in trainers and jeans, and then a teenager, dressed for a party, striking a pose. She collected them together, and carefully slid them back into the envelope.

"Thank you for bringing me these. I will treasure them." She sniffed, and wiped away a tear. "It's like watching you grow up. She was a pretty woman, your Janice. I can see why my husband wanted her. She was everything I am not. None of that matters now. She was kind to you. How did she die?" It was blunt.

"Cancer. She was only ill a short time, that I knew about, I think she didn't tell me straight away." Julia watched her mother think that through.

"She loved you. She was a good Mother. Maybe better that I was to Florian. Being a parent is difficult, you want the best for your children, but it is sometimes very hard to choose what the best is. I watched Florian make the same mistakes his father had made, and I had no idea what to do. If I could make any difference to where he was going. He's not a bad man. He has done bad things. I know that. It is hard to ignore what he is, and what he does. It's my fault that he is that way." She reached her hand across to take Julia's. "Did you love the man? Spencer?"

"Yes. I did, but he didn't love me. I never would have thought I would understand what my Father did to him. When I found out, what my ex-boyfriend had done, I thought I was OK, calm.

Then the friend, the one who was with my boyfriend, while he was still with me, the one who was moving in with him, wanted to talk to me, and I lost it. I'd never been that angry before. I wanted to hurt her, really do damage to her." She breathed, long and deep.

"You're a good girl. It doesn't matter if you're Anya or Julia, or Janices's girl, or mine. Whether you have the understanding in your blood, or whether you learned from Janice, doesn't matter. You are a good person, loyal, honest. I am proud of you." She patted Julia's hand. "Now I have to go to sleep. The treatment makes me tired more quickly. Today has been one of the best of my life." She pushed herself off the sofa and left Julia to think about what had happened.

The house was quiet. She felt she should tiptoe out to the super clean kitchen, to make herself a cup of tea. She slid her phone out of her back pocket.

"Ben? Hi. How was your day?" She caught her reflection in the window smiling into her phone and raised her eyes to the ceiling.

"Hi lovely Julia. How are you? Mick and I have just been discussing you." He laughed.

"The two of you have been talking about me behind my back?" She leaned against the worktop.

"You may as well know we have talked of very little else." He took a breath. "How's it going with your family?"

"It's been OK. Strange to finally have a family after all these years, but I like them, I wasn't sure that I would, but I do. My Father is different from how I expected, and it's all new, so they might decide they don't like me next week, but it's interesting. For all of us, maybe." She turned as the kettle clicked off.

"When do you think you'll be home? I'm asking on Mick's behalf, he's concerned." She could hear him smiling.

"Is he being good?" There was an uh huh noise at the other end of the phone. "I should be back tomorrow, that's the plan."

"Gemma wants you to ask your Father to come and talk to her."

"I'll ask. I have a feeling he won't be keen." She pulled the teabag out of the cup and carried it to the bin, with her hand cupped under the spoon in case it dripped on the floor. "I was wondering, one day, I mean, at some point, would you like to meet my mother?"

"Meeting the parents? I would like to. Do you think she would approve?"

"I told my Father I was seeing you, he seemed to think you were one of the good guys."

"That's a relief. Send him my best. I know this might sound strange, but he was genuinely a nice guy. I had a lot of time for him. I'm looking forward to seeing you tomorrow."

"Me too. Say hi to Mick for me?"

"I will. Sleep well my lovely."

"You too."

She carried her phone and her tea to the living room. She was too wired to sleep, and there was too much in her head that needed to be processed. She tucked her feet underneath her, and sipped her tea. The day had been too full, and way too emotional. Her Father had been a revelation, despite everything that she thought she had learned about him, although it had been implied rather than anything specific, she had expected a thug, but had met a sad and repentant man, who could now see where he had made mistakes. Could it be a pretence? Perhaps. Her Mother was, it surprised her, stronger than she had expected, she had spent years thinking about it and had worked it out. Whatever had happened between her parents, was their business, and they would work it out, or not, as they chose. Florian, she realized, worried her. He made her feel on edge, as though he was sitting on the edge of something, and he could tip over.

"Anya?" She jumped, she hadn't heard her Mother moving about. "Can't sleep?"

"No. Did I wake you?"

"No, I couldn't sleep either. Too much going on today. Is that tea? I'll make myself one, would you like another?" Julia shook her head and waited while the tea was made. The house was silent, no sound from neighbours or the street. It was a middle of the night silence. "It's a strange thing." She settled herself into the armchair. "I've waited for more than your lifetime for my husband to come back. He's the only man I ever loved. He's the only man I ever, anything." She laughed, hiding her mouth with her hand. "I have waited and waited, and now he's here, he is an old man. I watched him talking today and wondered how I felt about it all."

"Does he look very different? I thought Florian looked very like him." Julia sipped her tea, and wrinkled her nose at the cold taste. "They both have a feeling about them. A confidence, maybe?"

"They are both dangerous. Don't imagine that they are the pussy cats that they showed you today. They are both killers. I know it. I lived with both of them, protected, lied, hid, but that doesn't change who they are. I can love them and pretend to the world that they are better than that, but I can't lie to myself about them. You shouldn't either. Your Papa. What he did to your boyfriend? It was his pride, his humiliation, that pushed his anger over the edge. He was protecting you, but only because he sees his family as an extension of himself. That's what rage is. My husband and his son, they carry the rage." She sipped her tea.

Julia watched her carefully.

"Do you still love him?" It was said quietly, almost a whisper.

"Ah, there's the question. I wish I had an answer. They do too. I think a lot depends on what is decided." She watched her daughter, emotions and questions flitting their way across her face. "You show everything you feel. You need to stop that, if you can. It can be useful to know how you feel and not share it with the rest of the world." She nodded. "You're a smart girl."

"You're saying that Florian will kill him?" Julia sat forward, closer to her mother.

"If I can't forgive him, if he can't settle to a family life, if they can't find an agreement." She shrugged. "He can't go back to Cornwall, you have to see that, not with the Police finding that body. He can't go back to London, even if he wanted to, because people would be unhappy to see him back there. He can only stay in Florian's space if I accept him back, and he wants to come back to me. There is nowhere else for him to go. They both know it. You understand?" She wiped her hand over her face. Julia nodded. "I can tell you this, because you got it, straight away. You told me on the phone, warned me that the Police were looking to talk to both of them. You may not have grown up with this family, but you understand the loyalty that we demand of each other."

"What will you do?" Julia reached for her hand.

"I will think. Decide." She wrapped her soft fingers around Julia's hand. "You work hard with these hands. My Grandmother, she used to read the hands, when I was a child. She told me I would marry a bear. I laughed, but she told the truth." Her breath came out in a gentle sigh. "She had eight children, two died as babies, my mother was the only girl. My parents had three children, all girls. I was the lucky one, two children, one of each." She wiped a tear. "My beautiful girl." She smiled and swallowed. "You were such a perfect little one, you had almost no hair at all, but those eyes, oh my, you looked like my Grandmother, such a pretty little face." She shook her head. "Tell me about this Ben? Are you going to marry him?"

"Ha. It's early, only a few weeks. He's special. Kind, smart, gentle. Really good looking." She laughed, looking across at her mother from under her eyelashes.

"Sounds perfect. Maybe I can meet him?" She nodded. "This is nice, talking to my daughter about her boyfriend. I wish we had more time doing this, when you were growing up, but you have turned into a lovely woman. I wish I could thank your Janice, she must have been a lovely person, to bring up such a good daughter. Now I must sleep. Sorry darling girl." She patted Julia gently on her shoulder as she walked past, and Julia carried the two cups into the kitchen to wash up, and dry, before she followed her to bed, but not to sleep. What she had heard kept her mind racing and her eyes open.

35.

July 2018

"I want to talk to my Daughter, and my Wife." He watched Florian's reaction carefully. "Unless you have anything else planned for today."

"I don't have anything planned. I would like to see them too. We have some catching up to do. You and me too." He held the door open, watching every movement his Father made.

The car was fast, but not loud, not flashy. His son was not stupid, he was keeping his money and his business to himself. Slowly he nodded to himself, he was, in a corner of his mind, proud of his son. There was a part of him who knew how hard it was to come from nothing, and have money at your disposal, yet to restrain yourself from spending it, from showing off. That behaviour, beyond making the money, more than pulling himself and his mother out of poverty, into a better place, by his fingernails, and his fists, demanded respect.

"Nice car. I like it. Sensible." He nodded.

"Thank you." There was a smile, small and hard to see.

"I am only just learning how much I missed out on. I would have liked to see you when you were growing up. I know it was my choice, but you of all people know what my life was like. I want you to know, that I wish it had been different. I'm proud of what you have achieved, and how you looked after your Mama. Whatever happens between us. I know it might be that you decide that I should go. I'll always be proud of what you have done." He folded his hands in his lap and looked out of the window as they drove. The houses and shops sped past, as he watched and he waited for a response, he knew he had time to let what he had said sink in.

"My Mother, and my sister, are my responsibility. You have to understand, if either of them is made less safe, or less happy by your presence, then you will be removed. At the moment, both of them are happy that you want to be in their lives. You told me, in your letter to stay away from my sister, my clean, untainted Sister, but I am her brother, and I have a right to keep her safe. My Mother has been in my care since I was a very small child. I won't let you hurt her again. Just so long as we understand the rules." He stared straight ahead, watching his Father out of the corner of his eye.

"We understand. I get it. I want the same, I want to spend time with them. I'll do my best not to upset them. If I fuck it up, I'm sure you'll deal with it." He smiled to himself.

"We're here." He pulled into the driveway. His eyes traced up to the window, and, for the first time, his mother was not there waiting.

"I want to see some photos, of you when you were a child. Do you have some?" He turned in his seat to look head on at Florian.

"Mama has some. Ask her, she will be glad to show you." He opened the door, and stepped out. "She'll be waiting with cookies, or cake, or something. She loves to bake."

"She always did. She made me a cake, the day after our wedding. I was asleep, and I woke up to this smell, it was like heaven, sweet and warm and fruity. It pulled me out of bed and I found her in the kitchen. She'd got up early and baked. She baked with all her care and goodness. It's her way of saying she loves you." He pulled himself out of the car, leaning his weight carefully against the car. He watched his son weighing up how he carried his weight, how weakened he was. He closed the door of the car, and walked slowly to the door. He watched his son, as much. He knew he was strong, and young and fit. The only question was whether he was smarter than his Father. That remained to be seen. The spark, the excitement, he felt being back in a situation where he might win or lose everything, against an adversary he respected, pumped his adrenaline and raised his temperature. It gave him a taste for more.

They stopped at the door, and waited. Julia pulled it open.

"Good morning. How are you both today?" She stood back to let them in, and they followed her up the stairs. "We sat up late talking last night. So, we are just cooking breakfast. I'm trying to learn how to make pancakes. I warn you; it's not going well."

"Ah, your mother's pancakes. What a way to start the day." He rubbed his hands together, and climbed the stairs behind Florian.

"I have to go home tomorrow. While there is still a train strong enough to pull me there. I've done nothing but eat since I got here." She laughed, but swung into a chair and pushed a plate loaded with pancakes towards the two men sitting opposite her,

"I have some things to do today. Work things. I will trust you to stay here and talk." His eyes and his expression showed that Florian had no trust at all for his Father. "I will be back this afternoon."

"Thank you. For trusting me." They drank strong coffee, and ate tiny pastries and the pancakes.

An hour later Florian was gone, and the photographs were out again. Julia watched both her parents looking at children who had grown up away from them. Laughing together at their stories and the memories they had missed out on. It was something that she had never seen, she had watched Janice trace her fingers over the old photographs as though she could reach back through time to them, but Janice had nobody to share those memories, and neither had either of her parents, until now.

She made tea, and her mother made lunch, by dinnertime they were all wondering where Florian had got to, and none of them had any idea. They looked at each other, and the clock and then they looked at each other again. They drank more tea and passed cake to each other.

"I think we should check. Florian said afternoon. He wouldn't want me to worry he would call if he would be late. I will phone him." She checked the number in a tiny book and dialled. Her phone stood on a small table, and her back was towards them as she waited for an answer. "Florian. Please phone me, I am worried." She put the phone down and turned to them. "It's not like him. Something has happened."

"Where would he be? Do you know where he was going today?" Julia reached out to touch her. She shook her head.

"Give me his number." Her Father stood up, standing taller than he had before. She handed him the book. "This is too small." She handed him glasses. "OK. Do you have a laptop?"

"I do. I brought mine with me." Julia fetched it from the bedroom, and passed it to him. He sat, and opened it up. He opened a page and tapped in some numbers. She watched over his shoulder. "Can you trace a phone like this? Jesus, how do you even know how to do this?" He smiled, without turning away from the screen. "Did you find him?"

"Yes. I have the address where he is, it's in Moss Side, Manchester." He looked at her, and called up an address on Google maps. "It looks like an empty shop. We have to go there. Get him out."

"How? If you are saying that someone has him, he's not there for work, then they aren't going to let us in or let him out." She watched his face, and his eyes most of all.

"They won't want to, but you'll distract them, and I will get him out. Then we'll keep him safe, and not let him be in this kind of danger again. OK." His eyes held hers, and for that moment, for all that he was asking of her and for all that she knew he was, she trusted him, and she wanted to believe him that they could rescue her brother and keep him safe.

"I've never done anything like this, I would be less than no use at all. I would be too frightened. I would put both of you in danger." His hand was warm and his fingers wrapped around hers.

"I will tell you what to do. I will keep you both safe. All you have to do is to exactly what I tell you. It will be fine." She felt her head nodding, agreeing. "OK. You need a hat, something to cover your hair. You look too like him. Katya, find her a hat, come on, hurry." Her mother left the room. "You are going to be a cab driver. You will drive up to the front of this address, and knock on the door. I will tell you what to say. You must be brave. Think of cab drivers who have picked you up before, how they act, how they behave, put that in your mind. They are just wanting to get on with their day. That is what you should be. OK?" He rested his hand on her arm. "It will be fine. I have done this sort of thing before." He smiled, and she knew why Janice had loved him, and she knew that she would trust him, and why her mother, after years of waiting, and hardship, loved him still.

36.

She pulled up two streets away from the shop, and watched her father walk away, he had spent ten minutes collecting things from the house, so she knew he was armed. He walked slowly, as though he was an old man out for a stroll, no rush. She ran through in her head what he had told her, over and over. *Don't take shit, stick to the story, get as many as possible out the front to talk to her, and push for what she had to. Be a cabbie. Be a cabbie.* She waited until he was completely out of sight, then she counted slowly to a hundred, and slowly pulled the car away from the kerb. It was a new Ford, less than a year old. He had gone out and brought it back, she knew it was stolen, but she was past worrying about it. She forced her breath to be slow, and steady. She forced herself to think, to clear everything else. Be a cabbie, be a cabbie. That's all there is.

The row of shops was run down, a small newspaper shop, a post office, and a shop selling vape refills. The other three shops were boarded up, including the one she was headed to. She parked outside, there were plenty of spaces. She picked up the paper, and studied the address, as though it was new to her, and not burned on her brain. Aware that people may be watching her, she studied the paper, then checked the numbers on the doors. Shrugging to herself, she left the engine running and opened the door. There were no cars, nobody on the street. The front of the shop was boarded, and the windows above were dirty, the curtains hung thickly against them. She looked up at the windows, and checked her paper again.

She knocked on the door, and stood back, waiting for an answer. Nothing happened, and she waited, then remembering that she was a cabbie, she rang the bell, and knocked on the door. It pulled open fast, shocking her. The man who opened it wore a tight shirt, the sleeves straining against his biceps, and the neckline, against his thick neck.

"Hi. Cab. This is number 14, right? Picking up a package for Florrie Ann." She smiled.

"We didn't order no cab." Muscles was joined on the step by a smaller man.

"I don't know about that. I was asked to pick up a package for Florrie Ann. Is there a Florrie in there? Could you ask? I pick up a package under the same name most weeks, drive it wherever the man on the phone says. That's all I know. So I need the package. Come on, mate, I'm just here trying to do a job, I don't want to mess up your day. Can you just go and ask Florrie?" She planted her feet wide, steadying herself, like her Father had showed her. Another man joined them on the street, and pushed the others out of the way. He stepped into her, toe to toe.

"Go away." His breath was in her face, and he hadn't shaved, the skin on his face was scarred, and pitted, and very close to her eyes. He looked down into her face. Inside, in the pit of her stomach, something shook, she breathed through it, and held it still. She looked past him to the thinner man.

"Listen mate. Maybe you can help me. I'm a cabbie, booked by Florrie Ann, I'm supposed to pick up a package, that's all. I do it almost every week, pick it up, wherever they say, and drop it off, wherever they say. I don't want to be a pain, just want to earn my fare. Clock's ticking mate. Come on." She stood still. He pushed, she stood her ground. His breath was hot against her neck.

"No Florrie here. You've got the wrong address. Take my advice and go away." His eyes burned. Two more men stepped out onto the street behind him, joining muscles and his friend.

"Ok, let me look at the paper." She reached into her pocket, and pulled out the paper. "Look for yourself, this was the address that was given to me." She passed the paper to him. "That's here, right?" He studied the paper. Her phone rang in the car. "Ah, hold on, maybe that's my boss. One minute. She walked to the driver's door, and pulled it open. The name on her phone was Florian. "Hi?" She answered.

"Go. Now." Her Father's voice.

"It's my boss, sorry guys, wrong address. Have a good day." She smiled and slipped into the seat, driving slowly away.

Turning the corner, and taking the next turning, she spotted the two of them, and slowed next to them. The back door was pulled open, and Florian was pushed in, lying flat across the seats. Her Father jumped into the front seat faster than a man his age should move. "Drive." He said, and she pulled away.

Nobody said anything. She drove carefully, drawing no attention. From the back seat came an occasional moan. She glanced at her passenger, his knuckles were bloodied, and his breathing was ragged, but other than that he looked to be in good shape. She took a few wrong turns, but found her way back to her mother's house.

They helped Florian into the house, and Julia was horrified to see that he had been badly beaten and burned, blisters stood up on his arms and his neck. One of his fingernails was missing. They bathed his wounds and he slept on the sofa. She washed the blood from her father's knuckles, and ran the hot tap to fill the kitchen sink, plunging the kitchen knives he gave her into the water, and adding bleach as instructed, to clean them.

"You did well, I heard them talking, arguing about some mouthy cab driver." He laughed.

"Is Florian going to be OK?" She wiped the knives and put them back into the gaps they had left in the wooden block on the worktop.

"He will be, he's tough, but I want you to take him and your Mama back to Cornwall with you. I can't go back there, not now they found the body. I will be with you, but not now. The dust needs to settle here, Florian needs to be far away, and your Mama needs to be safe. You're strong, you'll care for them both, and we'll talk on the phone every day. I need to disappear for a while, OK?" She nodded. "I love you Julia. I love your Mama and Florian too. We worked well together today, didn't we?" She dried her hands and wrapped her arms around his waist. He raised his arms, and felt her head rest slowly against his chest. His hand cupped the back of her head, and he remembered holding her as a baby, her head resting in his hand. "Tell me you'll keep them safe."

"I will."

"Go now. Take the car to Bristol, then dump it and take the train. Look at me." Julia lifted her head. "Change lanes on the motorway often, watch behind you. Change just before an exit, see if anyone behind you does the same. OK?" She nodded. "Go. Take them." He turned away, and pulled on his jacket.

She went to the bedroom and picked up the bag she had packed earlier. Her mother was waiting by the door.

"We have to go. I'm taking you and Florian with me. We're going home." She smiled, and her Mama smiled right back.

37.

July 2018

Florian slept in the back of the car, while Julia drove. She did as she had been told, took the motorway, changed lanes a lot, dropped the two of them by the station, and parked three streets away, wiped the steering wheel, the gearstick and the door catches. The train rumbled them to Cornwall, and she was excited to be home. The cab from the station took them to her lane, and she opened the gate, so he could drive in. The sun was hot in the sky and the view was looking as beautiful as it ever did. She found that she was nervous, until she saw the expression on their faces.

"I love this. Your house is wonderful. This window. You build this?" Her Mother beamed at her.

"Glad you like it. We'd better get Florian inside." They helped him in, and she left them to settle in, glad to see that her bed was in the bedroom, and that there were walls now, no plaster, but definitely walls. They helped him to the bed, and she left her mother making tea. She pulled her phone out of her pocket and turned it on. She dialled Ben, and he answered on the third ring. "Hey. How are you?"

"I'm fine. What are you up to?" He sounded happy to hear from her.

"I'm home. I brought my Mum and Florian back with me for a visit." She watched her view out of the window. "I'd like you to meet them. Florian's in a bad way, but he's getting better."

"I'd love to see you, and there's a dog here, who has missed you."

"Come, the kettle's on."

"I'm on my way. Mick's already excited."

"Mama?" When did she get comfortable with calling her that? "Ben's on his way over, I'd like you to meet him, and he's bringing my dog home."

"Good that I brought cake with me then. Your cupboards are empty." She shrugged. "I looked."

Ben pulled up outside and she ran down to meet him, and to have Mick jump and squeak and squeal with happiness. She felt the same.

"Nice to see you. We missed you." He wrapped her in a hug, and leaned down to kiss her neck.

"Come and meet my family." She held his hand. "You should know, Florian got hurt, he's OK, but he will take a little while to heal up." Ben's forehead crinkled together.

"Was there an accident? Were you hurt?" His fingers tightened around hers.

"No. He had a disagreement with some business competitors, I guess. He's OK, mending." They walked together inside. "Ben, this is my mother." He held out his hand to her, and waited while she weighed him up. Slowly she took his hand.

"You make my daughter happy." It wasn't a question, it was a statement, or maybe an instruction. She passed him a plate with a piece of cake on it, and a cup of coffee. He sat where she pointed, and sipped his coffee. "I have been getting to know my daughter, and I like her. She's a kind, clever girl. She needs a good man. Are you a good man?"

"I am trying to be a better man. This cake is wonderful, did you make it?" He smiled, almost twinkling at her.

"Nice try, you can impress me, by making my daughter happy. I'll see if Florian is up. He would want to meet you. Since her Papa is not here." She fixed him with a good hard look.

"I guess I'd better make you happy then." He smiled a goofy smile and she giggled.

"Florian is coming to see you. I'll make him some tea." She rushed off to the kitchen.

"Hi." He limped into the room. "Sorry I look like this. My sister has been looking after me." He laughed. "My Father tells me that you're a good vet, and that I should be sure to say hello from him. He is dealing with some business interests and so he can't come back to Cornwall at the moment." He sat carefully on the chair, wincing as his body folded. "I wanted also to apologise for worrying you when I took my sister to see our mother, it was selfish and stupid of me. She explained it to me, but I was not ready to listen to her. I have learned a great deal recently. I have never been able to depend on my family before, and it's hard to learn to." He smiled, a genuine warm smile. "My sister is a good person, be nice to her."

"It's not going to happen again though, right." Ben met his eyes, and held them.

"No. Not ever."

"I promise I will be nice to her. I am a bit worried about you though. Did you see a doctor about those injuries? That finger is very red, it might be infected. Did you disinfect the wound?" he looked at Julia.

"We washed all the wounds, with water and disinfectant, and then we covered them. Then we came back here, so he's been in the train, which might be a bit grubby and a cab." She chewed her lip.

"No doctors." Florian looked fierce. "Can you fix it?"

"I'm a vet, not a doctor." He shook his head. "But, I suppose, a family member, who is injured, I could. OK." He shrugged off his jacket. "Julia, do you have, no, you won't. I'll use things from my car." He brought his bag in, and started to pull off the dressings. "OK, this one on your finger is infected, and this one, and this. Let's start with your finger." Gently he cleaned the nail bed. "This looks really painful. How did you do it?" He wiped and cleaned. Carefully he replaced the dressing with a new and much more professional one. Then he moved to the blisters on his arms and then his neck. "Julia, could you get Florian a drink please?" He watched her leave. "OK. I think you've taken a heavy beating, and I'm guessing someone burned you with a cigar. The fingernail, I think must have really hurt. I suspect that's why you don't want a doctor to look?" Florian nodded. "Are the people who did this likely to show up here?" Florian shook his head. "Are they likely to want to hurt Julia?"

"Definitely not. It was business. I'm out. Not going back. I'll get a place for my Mum down here, and then decide what to do. Thank you for doing this. I promise you, Julia won't come to any harm because of me." His eyes met Bens. "I didn't see this coming. I was betrayed by someone I thought was my friend. I've been stupid, I'm lucky to be out."

"OK. All done. Try to drink a lot of water and sleep. I can't give you any anti biotics. You're fit, you should recover, if you take the time to let your body rest. I'll check with you in a couple of days. Let them fuss and take care of you." He nodded, and smiled. "If you were a dog, I'd pat your head about now. I'd give you a biscuit too." They both laughed.

38.

"Julia. I know that life has been complicated for you lately, and I am trying not to be difficult about this, but I am running a murder investigation. A man has been killed, I think because he cheated on you, and I believe by your father. I need to talk to him, Julia. Please tell me where he is." Gemma leaned her elbows heavily on the table between them. "Please."

"Gemma, I'm being honest with you. I last saw him in Manchester, my brother was in trouble, we went to help him. Then we three came down here, so Florian could heal up his injuries. My Father stayed behind. I don't know where he went from there. I have no number for him." She wiped her hand across her face. "If he calls, I promise I will let you know."

Her phone rang. "Hang on a minute Julia." She stepped outside and Julia watched her talking, walking, and waving her arms. She hung up the phone and took a breath steadying herself and gathering herself, before opening the door again. "Did you know?"

"What?" Her eyebrows squeezed together.

"He's done a bloody deal, for immunity. I can't touch him." Her voice shook a little. "Julia, I have an almost watertight case against him for the murder, and he knows it. Shit, shit, shit." She took a long breath. "I'm going home." The door shut behind her, and she walked, as though she would leave boot prints in the driveway.

"He did a deal?" Florian lifted an eyebrow.

"You were listening?"

"Yeah." He sat down on the sofa, and rested his head back against the cushions, and closed his eyes.

"I don't have any way to contact him, so we'll have to wait to hear what he has to say when he decides to ring us." She sat next to him. "How are you feeling?"

"Your vet is a good doctor." He smiled. "Or perhaps I am more like a dog than a human. I want to know what sort of deal he did." Florian turned towards the window at the noise of a car engine. "That's my car." Florian walked to the window. "It's him. I don't believe it." Julia joined him at the window to watch their father climb out of the car.

Julia ran to the door. "Hello. You found us."

"I would find you no matter where you were, nothing clever about it, I called Ben at the surgery and asked him not to spoil the surprise." He wrapped an arm around her. "How are you, Florian? You look better."

"The police were here, they said you did a deal. What did you give them?" Florian leaned against the side of the sofa. "It must have been something big, to get off a murder charge."

"I gave them the names, of everyone I did business with, for years, it will save them years of work that would get them nowhere. I told them about the supply chain we created and the distribution we organized. They will clean up. I will be very unpopular. I know that. I am going into witness protection. They are changing my name, like they think I don't know how to do it myself." He laughed, and squeezed Julia.

"Will you have to relocate?"

"Yes. I'm going to live in Cornwall. I think we should all do that." He smiled over their heads. "Katya, I wanted to ask if you would give me another chance. Not because you think it would keep me alive, if Florian thought we were together, yes, darling, I knew that was what you thought. I'm asking for a chance to make it up to you."

"I don't know. I might not like you anymore, you're an old man now." She smiled.

"Think about it, don't decide straight away. I'm just glad to be here with my children and my wife, and feeling like I have a future." He rested his hand on Florian's shoulder. "OK?" His eyes locked with his sons, and he waited to see a small nod of Florian's head. "Ben is coming over later, I suggested we go out to the pub near his surgery, they do good food, so your Mama can take a break from cooking, and we can all talk together, like a family." He clasped Julia's hand between both of his. "Now, will you show me your place?" She nodded, and took him through the house.

When they were upstairs, and away from the others, he held his hand out to her. "Julia, I want to say this, away from the others. I am sorry about your boyfriend. I was wrong. I am so proud of you, and what you have done. I am glad you had Janice, she was a lovely woman, far too good for me, a lot like your Mama. She did me the biggest favour when she took you away from me, you were safer and in a better place than you would have been. Missing out on you growing up was my punishment, and I see now how much I missed out on, with you, and with Florian. Honestly though, the other day, when you stood on the pavement and kept everyone busy so I could get him out, it was brave and surprising. I wouldn't have asked you to do it, if I had any other choice." He looked out at her view. "This is amazing. Clever of you."

There was a noise downstairs, footsteps thundered through the living room and up the stairs. The dog launched himself from the top of the stairs, squealing and crying, his eyes bright and his tongue hanging out in excitement.

"Looks like Mick missed you." Julia laughed. She knew he was her father's dog. If she had any doubt, Mick's reaction would have been enough proof for anyone. A tear escaped from her eye. She was second best. Her father knelt on the floor and put his arms around his dog.

"Enough, enough. Calm down." The dog sat next to him, leaning into him, happy yelps still escaping occasionally. "Julia, he looks wonderful, so healthy. Do you know how my chickens are? My cow?"

"I don't know. Ben might." Mick finally saw her, and padded over to say hello. "Hello boy. You found your real owner now, huh? Good boy. It's OK. I'll miss you, but I can see you whenever I visit my dad. OK?" She ruffled his ears. "Good lad. Go on." She turned away, for some reason she didn't want either her dad or the dog to see how hurt she was.

"You don't have to miss him, he's yours."

"No, he was always yours, I was just looking after him while you were away. We had some fun, but he was never mine." She wiped away the tear that fell.

"Sweetheart, they're never ours, only on loan, and they always break your heart, that's the deal." He held out his hand, and she took it. "Come on Mick." The three of them got downstairs as Ben arrived. "Ben, hello. My favourite vet. How are you?"

"Good, Mr Alex." He held out his hand to shake, "I see Mick has found you."

"Alex, please." He bypassed the handshake and wrapped Ben in an awkward hug. "I need to speak to you." He pulled away. "Ben and I are going to take Mick for a walk around your land, and then we can go out and get something to eat. OK?" He patted his leg and Mick followed him, Ben followed him too, and they walked away from the house up towards the woods. "What happened to my chickens Ben, and my cow?"

Ben stopped walking and looked straight at him. "I'm really sorry, to have to tell you, but they died. I didn't tell Julia all about it, I couldn't at the time, it was a professional matter, I was called in by the police, because you were missing and the animals were dead." He swallowed, watching the expression on the face in front of him change. "The police called me in because they wanted a vet's opinion on what happened to the animals."

"What was your opinion?" His voice shook.

"That someone had cut the throat of your cow, and the chickens I wasn't sure about. They were pretty badly decomposed. The lab results said that they had been fed some kind of foam that swells up when it gets wet. That was what killed them." He stood very still, watching the man in front of him try to collect himself.

"Thank you for being so direct, and honest with me. I am grateful. I need a few minutes to get myself together, then we will go for dinner. OK?" He walked away, without waiting for an answer, with Mick padding at his heel.

39.

"Florian. Can I speak with you for a moment? Just before we go out to eat." He held the door open, and waited for Florian to join him outside. "Do you want to tell me why?" His voice was low, quiet, but there was an edge to it.

"What do you think I know?" Florian straightened his spine, and met his father's glare.

"The day you came to my home, armed and raging, you pointed a gun at my head, and told me to get into the boot of the car. Which I did. You were on your own, you did some things. I want you to tell me what you did." He stepped closer to his son.

"I went through your house, and took some documents, a necklace which had Julia in diamonds, the deeds to houses, and some other bits and pieces."

"My chickens, my cow?"

"Ah, yes. I'm sorry about them. I was angry. I shouldn't have done that. I suppose you are lucky the dog wasn't around." He reached out and ruffled the dog's ears.

"I should kill you. If you were anyone else, I would. As we stand, I will not discuss this with your sister or your mother, but let me tell you, right now, you are not a son I can be proud of. Stay out of my way, I don't trust you around anyone or anything I care about." He walked to the front door, and pulled it open. "Ladies? Ben? Are you ready? Then we had better get going. The table is booked."

Florian had very little to say over dinner, the atmosphere was tense over the starters and the mains arrived with a side of family stress and trauma.

"OK. What's going on between you two?" Julia put down her fork and spoke under her breath. "Whatever it is, we are a family, so we all talk about it." She rested her elbows on the table, and looked directly at her father. "Janice always said, a family that talks to each other, gives each member strength, you know she was smart, so let's take her advice, shall we?"

"Julia."

"No. No more secrets. What has Florian done to upset you? He's behaving like a sulky teenager, and you're looking as though he might not make it to dessert. I don't care which of you tells me, but one of you, please." She waited.

"Julia, I did something really angry. Our father found out about it today. I should have told him about it before. It was a stupid, childish thing to do, and destructive. I have apologized, but I know I have hurt him. I will try to make it up to him." He reached his hand out to lay it over hers. "Ben told our father, before I got the chance."

"I asked Ben what happened and he told me. He didn't know it was you, he only knew it happened." He folded his napkin. "Julia. I told Florian I would not discuss this with you, and I won't. If he chooses to tell you, I can't stop him." His eyes were hard as stone chips.

"Is everything OK with your meals?" The waitress was cheery and all smiles.

"Wonderful. Thank you." He beamed at her.

"Florian? Tell me. Please." Julia turned to him in her seat.

"I killed his precious animals. I killed his chickens, his cow, and if I had seen it, I would have killed his dog. I was angry, I wanted to hurt him, but I couldn't. I've never understood why people could love animals. Stupid. What's the point? Look how you ran and cried when the dog ate that poisoned meat. You were more upset about the stupid dog than you were about Mama being sick. You and him, you're the same, you love the animals, but you don't care about people. You don't care about me and Mama." Florian was sucking air in as though he had run a mile.

"How did you know Mick ate poisoned meat?" Her voice was low, and angry.

"How do you think? I watched from your woods. You, and your dog, loving each other, and then him, the vet, like the perfect picture. Like he said." His finger pointed at their Father. "You were clean, untouched by the work he and I did. He begged me to stay away from you, leave you to your safe, happy life. Crawl back into the gutter, like the rat he made me. What choice did I have, but to be a rat, when he left me in the sewer to grow up? How else was I supposed to protect my Mama, when she was left alone in the world? You made me what I am, old man. Now you see what you have made and you don't like it." His Mother reached out a hand and rested it on his arm, but he shook it off. He was too angry to be calmed.

"You poisoned Mick?" He huffed out a laugh, and pushed his chair out, staggering a little as he walked away. "How could you?" Tears were overflowing her eyes.

He turned towards her. "Stay with your family Julia, you are more welcome than I am."

"Bill please." Her Father stood up. "Come on, sorry, I've lost my appetite." He threw notes on the table, and walked away.

"Julia. Stay with me tonight, let them sort out their argument. We can be in my flat in less than a minute." Ben held her hand, his eyes hard. "I didn't know it was Florian, who hurt your dad's animals. I don't know if I would have done anything differently if I knew."

"Come on, let's see how they are getting on." She wiped a finger under her eye.

Outside, Florian was already gone. Her parents were speaking low in their own language. "Where did he go?"

"Julia, I don't know. He's angry. Let's let him cool off a bit, OK?" He smiled over her head at Ben. "Sorry Ben, to drag you into the family nonsense."

"I'm going to stay at Ben's tonight. Give you some space to work out what happens next. Perhaps you're right about letting him calm down, but I'm worried about him." Ben held her hand and they waved their goodbyes. Her parents looked like any other older couple, sitting side by side in the car, and they made her smile when she looked back at them.

Ben's flat was only across the road. And he was right they were back there within the minute. He let them in, and turned on the lights, taking her jacket, and letting her sit down, before pouring her a glass of wine and settling on the couch next to her.

She turned to him, her neck tilted against his arm, and met his mouth halfway. He kissed her, and her body warmed to him. There was a noise, something moved in the room with them, making them both turn to look. Florian was leaning against the door frame.

40.

July 2018

"Hello. I wondered if you might decide to stay over again." He pushed his back away from the wooden frame and walked over to the other sofa. "I was thinking about the last time we were all here together, the night you stayed over, and I waited outside. I watched families eating where we just were, and I wondered what it was like to have people around you who cared. In the morning, I picked you up and we went to see Mama, remember?"

"Yes. I remember. Why did you kill the animals, Florian?" Her voice was a little shaky.

"Because I couldn't kill him. I went there, thinking I would. I had a gun, some knives, plenty of stuff. But when I looked at him, I decided I didn't want to. I didn't know what to do. So I told him to get in the boot of the car, and I had a look through his house. Found the stuff I gave you, some other things. Then I went outside, and the chickens were there, just clucking about, like the idiots I always knew they were. I had a bag of building foam stuff in the back of the car, left over from filling a gap at my house. I pulled a handful out and chucked it for them. The stupid things ran about fighting each other to get hold of it." He laughed, shaking his head at the memory. "So I threw some more. It swells up, when it gets wet, so I suppose it didn't do them any good. There was a cow, standing looking at me, I was laughing at the chickens, and I just thought; why should he love them, and not love his son? I was angry, hurting. So I killed the cow. I cut it." He ran his finger across his own neck.

"He saved your life. Last week. He risked his own life to save you. He didn't hesitate, because you're his son, and I'm your sister. We came and got you, because you were in trouble. That's what families do." She sat forward, pushing her hair out of her face. "Can't you see that he loves you? Both of them do."

"Not anymore." He hung his head.

"That's not true. He's angry, but he will calm down." Her eyes met his as he raised his head. "It might take a while." She chewed her lip.

"Yeah. I'm a bit fucked up."

"Yeah, I guess you are." She thought about it. "What was your plan when you left his place, with him in the boot?"

"I didn't have one. Not then, I couldn't kill him. I couldn't let him loose. I just drove. I ended up back in Manchester, I took him to a house, I use sometimes, and paid a junkie to look after him, so I could think about it."

"Think about it?"

"About what to do. I had some clues, about where to find you, so I went looking for you. All the time I was in Cornwall, he was in Manchester. I didn't go and see him until after Mama came out of hospital. I was still deciding whether I should kill him, to be honest. Then when I knew you were coming up, and Mama was so excited, I thought, why not, maybe it might be a good thing to find out if we could all get on, if we could be something, some sort of family. If I'm honest, I'd forgotten about the animals." He picked at a nail. "I watched Mama, I knew she wanted to have him back, it's all she ever wanted, but she was weighing it up. She was watching me, to see what I would do. She knew, I think, that if it didn't work, with that body turning up on his land, there was nowhere else he could go. He definitely knew. He was watching me too. Every night when I dropped him back to his room, and locked the door, I walked away and I knew he was wondering, just like I was, whether this was going to work. When he turned up in that back room in Moss Side, I'd never been so pleased to see anyone. I would have died there. No question. He took three of them out, young fit guys, then half carried me out of the back door." He raised his eyebrows.

"So, what are you going to do?" She leaned forward, her head slightly tipped to the side.

"I'm going to see him in the morning. Try and make it up to him. I don't know, maybe buy him some chickens." He shrugged his shoulders.

"Replacing them won't fix it. Anymore than replacing your Father with your Uncle worked for you. It's about how we feel about someone isn't it, and how they feel about us? You said you didn't understand why I love the dog. Why? You understand how people care about each other, animals are the same. That's all it is."

"Can I sleep on your sofa Ben?"

41.

The morning was dull, with clouds gathering and pushing across the sky. As the first few drops fell fat and heavy on the windscreen, Ben pulled on to the drive outside Julia's house. He drove away leaving Florian and Julia to fix the problems in their family. Julia fished out her keys and opened the door, before they got soaked.

Mick was pleased to see them, and bounced around Julia, while she stroked his soft head. Her parents were sitting at the table, with the remains of breakfast in front of them. They looked happy, and for the first time, she saw them as a couple, just doing an ordinary thing, just drinking tea and eating some toast, and that being enough. It hadn't been something she had considered.

"I'm sorry. Julia has explained a lot to me, and I've thought about stuff most of the night. I wanted to say sorry, really. I mean it. Tell me what I can do to make this better." He leaned against the sofa as he spoke.

"We have been talking about this too. We have come up with a plan. You might not like it, but we think it will be good for you. I am going to speak to some people, and then you and I are going out, son." He nodded, and went upstairs.

"What is the plan?" Florian sat down to the table and took a piece of toast.

"It's a surprise, and you might enjoy it. It will be hard work, and you will need to try hard to get it right, to earn back the respect you lost. Do you want butter?" He nodded and she pushed it across the table to him. He spread the butter and took a bite, as their Father joined them.

"Come on. Let's go." Florian raised an eyebrow at his sister, and followed him outside.

"Tea?" Julia nodded, and took the cup.

"What are they going to do?"

"We will go to see them this afternoon, and find out." Her Mother looked secretive, and happy.

"You look happy today. Is it going well with him?" She sipped the tea.

"Yes. Really well, I had forgotten a lot of things about him that I missed. He's a good man, and I believe him that he's sorry for what he did. To all of us." She reached across the table and covered her daughter's hand. "I am going to start looking for somewhere for us to live. Me and your Papa. We need a new place, and some time to see if this is a mistake or not. Florian will be moving too. You and Ben will have your house back."

"Ben doesn't live here." Her brows knitted together.

"He will though, in time? You have more work to do too, to get the other buildings ready, and you need to get holiday people here." She rubbed the back of Julia's hand. "Have some toast too."

"Where is Florian moving to?"

"Ah, you are going to visit him there this afternoon. Come on, I want you to show me the woods, once you finish here. We can take Mick." She left Julia to finish her breakfast, while she fetched a coat, and boots, and then together they walked up the hill towards the woods and watched Mick running in mad circles around them. "Oh, this smell, the smell of trees in the rain, I remember this from when I was a child. It's wonderful." She reached for Julia's hand. "I know you're angry with your brother, it must hurt that he stood in these woods and watched you, and that he poisoned your dog, but he is a bit broken inside. He needs to mend, and he will, if we give him time." She watched the rain, as it fell across the land between them and the house. "I've spent a lot of time waiting, and I think, now, that it has been worthwhile. Look at that rain, it used to be part of the sea, now it's part of the air, and when if lands, it will be part of the earth, then it will drain out of the land, into the rivers, and be part of the sea again. We can be like that too, lovely Anya." There was no sound except the dripping leaves above them for a little while, and Julia considered her mother, and what she had said. "Come on, let's get back and get dry, I want to make a picnic for us all before we go."

She gave Julia a small piece of paper once they were in the car, with a postcode and a name on it. Playing along, she set the sat nav and drove. Her Mother was still smiling quietly to herself, and they had left Mick sleeping happily in the house. The rain had cleared and washed most of the clouds, leaving only a few fluffy white ones chasing across the sky. The drive was short, and within a few minutes she pulled in through a gateway. The driveway opened onto a yard, with a house on one side, and some outbuildings on the other. She parked the car, and they climbed out.

"Are you sure this is the right place?" Julia looked around the yard, and turned back to her mother.

"Oh yes. Come on." She bustled towards the house, and opened the door. "Hello?" She shrugged, and went over to the outbuildings, just as Florian came out.

"Mama. Hello." His face was red and sweaty, he had been working hard. "Come and see." They followed him back into the small building. In a corner, there were hay bales, lit with big heat lamps. In the middle were tiny yellow fluffy chicks. "Look. We got them this morning. They're only a few days old." He scooped one up, and showed them, then gently put it back in with the others. He showed them the paddock at the back of the property and the fences they had repaired. "I am going to do this. I have some time now, while I get better, and I can raise these chickens, and learn about them." He looked younger, happier and more open to the future. "I thought when I got here, that I would hate it, but you know what? It was good. I enjoyed the work, and that you could see something changing, putting it right."

"I took a lot longer to learn that, and I wished I learned it earlier, but I got there in the end, and so will you." The body language between them had changed, since the day before. They ate the picnic, and gave Florian some more bags of shopping, and left him to it.

Julia left her parents with Jonty who was happy to show them every property he had, and she drove herself down to the beach.

Amanda was sitting at the coffee bar, and she jumped when Julia sat down next to her.

"Am. I think you deserved everything I said, and more, but I don't like how it made me feel, so we have to work out a way to sort this." She watched Amanda order two coffees, and sat back against the seat.

"I am sorry. I have no excuses." Amanda reached across the table slowly, her hand stopping just an inch from Julia's.

"I know. He's dead Amanda. He was a bit of an idiot, and he probably didn't deserve to die, but we are here, we can't change the truth. I don't know if I'll ever trust you, or be friends with you, but I don't want to hate you, or be angry anymore." The coffee arrived and it was good, and hot.

"I'll take that." She sipped and watched the water for a while.

"Did he die because of me?" Her voice was tiny, less than a whisper.

"No. He died because of him, Amanda. He pissed off the wrong person. Stop beating yourself up, or don't, it's up to you, but I am going to stop, right here, and move on. I've got too much to do and enjoy, to waste time being angry anymore." Julia reached the inch between them, and wrapped her fingers around Amanda's. "Thanks for the coffee, Am." She stood and walked away feeling lighter and better than she had for a while. In her imagination, and without looking back, she saw Mike and Amanda sitting at the table, watching the sea, and drinking good coffee, and she wished them well.

42.

The sun rose over her view, as she sipped her coffee. She had crossed to the window and watched the sky change from a strip of light on the horizon to a blaze across the clouds. There were sounds behind her but she kept her head still, not wanting to miss the best show in town. A wet nose on her ankle confirmed her suspicion that the puppy was awake.

"Hello baby. How are you today?" She knelt to ruffle his ears. His soft brown eyes were wide and alert. He would look a lot like Mick when he grew up. "Do you want to go outside? Come on then." She opened the door and watched the pup sniff and search, and finally find a spot to pee, before trotting back to the house, in search of breakfast and a cuddle.

"Hey, don't close the door on me!" Her brother walked up the driveway. "I have eggs." She stood back to let him in, then closed the door to leave the cold outside.

"Is that your way of inviting yourself to breakfast?" She stroked the pup's head and then straightened up to take the eggs from him.

"Yes. Is Ben up?" He knelt on the floor and played with the puppy, receiving excited barks and tail wagging as a reward. "Good boy." She watched them together, and marvelled at the change in him. He had taken to the farm, raising his chickens, and adding goats too. He had even accepted the community service order that had been plea bargained for him by their father on the charges brought against him for killing the chickens and the cow.

"He will be, as soon as he smells the eggs cooking." She started to break the eggs into a bowl, listening to him chatting with the dog.

"Are you still OK to have Christmas here?" He stood up and laughed at the puppy's dancing and jumping to try to get him to play. "I'm looking forward to it."

"Mama will want to cook, so we have compromised, we have more space, so they can come and stay a couple of days before, and she can use the kitchen." She pulled a loaf of bread out of the cupboard. "You're coming to stay too?"

"You know I can't, the chickens don't know it's Christmas time. I'll be here for Christmas Eve though, and for Christmas Day." He watched her cook.

"I'm going up to the woods later to pick out a tree, Ben said he'd cut it for me on the weekend. I'm looking forward to it." She popped the bread into the toaster. "I'm glad you're going to be here for Christmas."

"Me too."

"Me three." Ben wrapped his arms around her. "Morning Florian. Are you on my list this morning?"

"Yes. I need you to check them, just to be sure."

Julia pushed plates with toast and steaming eggs at each of them, and a cup of tea each.

"Thank you darling. I may as well take Florian with me, and start my list with him. I'll be home before three, let me know if you need me to bring anything back." He kissed her gently and closed his eyes to thank his lucky stars that this woman was who he came home to.

"I have visitors coming to stay in number three today, so I've got lots to do. I'll see you later." She watched them jump into Ben's car and waved them off.

She walked the dog, then went to check on the holiday let, there was very little left to do, just a few last checks. She was pleased with the way the small lets had come out. Both with two bedrooms, and an open plan kitchen living room. She had fitted out the space with a small dining table and two sofas, and decorated in soft creams and pale pastels. They were beautiful, and she was proud of them.

The visitors, Mr and Mrs Jenson, arrived just after two, and she showed them the section of the house, where they would be staying. She left them to settle in, and went back to her house, where she was planning on making a cup of coffee. Two steps before she reached the door, she heard footsteps behind her, and turned, wondering if there was something that she had forgotten to explain to her guests. Mr Jenson put both his hands out, and pushed her hard against the wall, the stones rough against her back. The air wooshed out of her mouth, leaving her gasping.

"Where is Florian?" She found that he was out of focus, as she struggled to drag a breath into her lungs.

"I don't know. He was here two weeks ago, but he's travelling, he was catching a flight the day he left here." The stonework was hard against her back.

"Phone." He held out his hand. She reached into her back pocket, pulled out her phone and passed it to him. She watched him scroll through her phone. He passed the phone to her. Florian's number was on the screen. "Speak to him, tell him he needs to come back." She pressed the button.

"Hi this is Florian, leave me a message." She held the phone out.

"It's gone to voicemail." She hung up. "Shall I try his girlfriend?"

"Show me the number before you dial." He growled. She scrolled carefully through the numbers, found Gemma, and showed the screen to him. He nodded.

"Hello Gemma, it's Julia. I'm not sure if Florian is with you? It's just some people he knows have turned up at mine and they're looking for him. I've rung him, but it's gone to voicemail. It's important I reach him." She held her breath, hoping that Gemma would understand.

"Julia. Hi. He's not here right now, but he won't be long, I'll get him to call you when he gets back. Are you OK? You sound out of breath." Her voice sounded a little stilted, but maybe only if you had heard her talk normally.

"Yes, just a bit stressed. You know me, always rushing about at the house." She waited.

"OK, leave it with me. If I don't see him in the next hour, I'll phone you back, OK? I'll see you soon. Take care." The line went dead. Julia hoped that Gemma was on the way, and that she was bringing friends. Her phone rang in her hand. Florian's name showed on the screen. She turned the phone to show him. He nodded.

"Hello? Florian. I'm sorry, I know you'll be in France by now, but some friends of yours have booked into the holiday let. They want to talk to you. They're insisting. I know it will take you a couple of days to get back, but I think you should come. Oh, I left a message with Gemma when I couldn't get through to you earlier, I hope that's OK." She took a breath, waiting for her brother to please, please catch up with her.

"Hiya. Yeah, France is lovely. Which friends turned up?" She could hear his breathing.

"Do you want to speak to him?" She held the phone out to the man in front of her. He took it from her.

"Florian, I don't care where you are, get here. I'm not known for my patience. Your sister's a pretty girl. Don't make me think up ways to pass the time." He passed the phone back to her.

"Gemma will help you pack up quickly and get home. I know you can't get here today, but as fast as you can. OK? Safe journey home. Do you remember Mum used to say that to me? We talked about it the other day." She pushed back against the wall.

"Yes, she used to say, 'safe journey home, because you're coming home to your Mum.' I remember. I'll be home soon. Keep it together." The phone went dead in her hand. He held his hand out, and she put the phone into it.

She let him pull her to her feet and offered no resistance when he pushed her towards the holiday let. She hoped that she had people coming who would help, there was no need to, no point in pushing this man to be angry or violent to her.

"How do you know my brother?" She sat on the sofa, which she had chosen, and whose cushions she had plumped, and tried to make conversation with the man who scared her. He ignored her.

"Hey, Laura, he didn't hang about, he has a new girlfriend, looks like you got dumped." He smirked. The woman squirmed, and pulled the hoodie she was wearing tight across her chest. He pointed his finger at Julia. "Don't be sitting there thinking he'll be back, like some hero in a movie."

Julia rested her head back against the cushion and said nothing. She knew Florian was less than ten minutes away by car, and that Gemma would be here soon. She could wait.

"Make a coffee, Laura. Come on, shift yourself." The woman pulled herself off the sofa, and filled the kettle. She raised a cup at Julia, offering her a cup. Julia shook her head, but smiled her thanks.

The man opened a bag and found a sandwich and a packet of crisps. He opened the packaging, and when the coffee was made, he tucked in with gusto. "Don't worry, I won't hurt you, so long as you do as you're told. I don't want you, just him."

They sat in silence after that. Julia sat on one sofa, while Laura sat on the other. The man sat at the table, even after he finished eating.

Julia's phone rang after what felt like hours but was perhaps twenty minutes. The screen said it was her mother calling. The man checked it, and passed her the phone.

"Make it quick, get rid of her."

"Hello?"

"Hello darling. How are you today?" Her Mother's voice was cheery, there was no sign that Florian had contacted her.

"I'm a bit busy today, I've got people just arrived for the holiday let." She tried to keep her breath steady.

"Yes, your Papa told me, he said Florian is coming back from holidays." There was a pause, Florian had been in touch with them. Her Father was coming to help her.

"Yes, I spoke to him earlier. I need to get on, there's lots to do today. Can I call you later?" Julia waited for a reply.

"Are you still cleaning in the holiday let?"

"Yes, not much left to do now." Julia breathed out, they wanted to know where she was. They were coming for her. She would be OK.

"OK darling, speak to you later. Love you, Julia." Her Mother never called her anything but Anya. This was a message.

"Love you, Mum." She hung up the phone and he took it back.

"So how come you're looking for Florian?"

"Mind your business. Laura. Come and sit with her. I want to be able to keep an eye on both of you." He pointed at the other side of the sofa, and Laura crossed the room, staying as far away from him as she could.

She was a pretty girl, but there was something closed and scared in her eyes. Julia wanted to reassure her, tell her that Gemma was only a pretend girlfriend, but then, maybe there were other reasons why she was afraid.

Julia's phone rang. He looked at the screen. "It's your brother." He passed the phone to her.

"Florian? How's it going?" She watched the man's face.

"I've got a booking for the ferry. I'll have to drive all night, but I reckon I can be back to you late morning tomorrow. Let him know." There was an echo on the line as though he was in the car.

"He can hear you, it's on speaker."

"OK. So, I'm setting off now. I'll phone you when I get to the ferry terminal, and let you know, but I'm aiming to catch the five o'clock boat. How are you holding up? Are you OK?" Five. Something was happening at five.

"Stay safe, Laura and me are fine. Your friend wants to talk to you, not us." She swallowed to moisten her throat. "Sorry, I had to call Gemma, so Laura knows you have been seeing someone, I didn't mean to upset anyone."

"Don't be sorry, I'll talk to Laura when I get there, and explain. Do what he tells you, and I'll come and straighten this out. OK?" He was on his way. She just needed to hold on to that.

"OK. See you tomorrow." She listened to him cut off the line, and checked the time on her phone. It was nearly three, he had told her five in the morning, but she thought it must mean they would be there at five this afternoon, perhaps it would be dark then, that might help them to get closer without being seen. Her mind raced with the new information, and she hardly noticed when he took the phone from her.

She started to count, slowly as she could in her head. Trying to work out how long had passed. The silence gathered around the three of them, leaving her space to count, to trying to keep track. When she imagined it was nearly half past, and long enough had gone by she licked her lips.

"Are you guys hungry? I haven't eaten since breakfast." She tried to look as though she had thought about it just then. "I could order pizza. There's a company that delivers in Constantine Bay. The number's on my phone, if you like pizza, that is."

"I could eat some pizza. I'm hungry." Laura's eyes flicked closed.

"For fucks sake. Why don't we get a few beers, have a party?" His tone was aggressive, angry. "Fine. Order a fucking pizza." He threw the phone at the gap between them and she grabbed it.

"Any toppings you like especially?" She scrolled through the numbers.

"No anchovies or pineapple. Other than that, I don't care." He turned away.

"I like black olives and onions with those spicy peppers." Laura smiled at her, and waited for her to make the order.

She pulled up the number. "Hi, can I order two pizzas please, on my account, my name is Julia and I'm at Trethian Farm. Yes. Yes. Can I have a spicy veggie pizza, and a meat feast? And some drinks, Coke, two litres and a large bottle of water. Can you deliver, what time? Yes, five is OK. I'm in the holiday let, right across from where you normally deliver. Great, see you then." She hung up, then quickly scrolled with her thumb and pressed the dial button, hanging up again straight away. She held the phone out to him, and sat back. "They don't have a driver til five. I know it's a wait, but it'll be worth it, they do good pizza. Meantime, shall I make us a cup of tea or coffee? I put some milk in the fridge for you, and some tea bags and coffee, earlier." When I thought you were ordinary visitors, she smiled to cover the thought that must have been written across her face.

"Fine, make coffee. Not you, Laura."

43.

November 2018

"It's nearly five, shall I find some plates in the cupboard?" Laura stood up and went into the kitchen, there were some noises of doors opening and closing and the clink of crockery and glasses.

Julia watched Laura setting the table, and waited. He turned in his chair and watched her.

"What are you waiting for?" His voice was harsh in the quiet of the room.

"Pizza. I'm hungry. We're all waiting for something aren't we? You're waiting for Florian to sort out whatever it is you're angry about. I'm not sure what Laura's waiting for." She closed her eyes and wondered what the time was. Not knowing was making the waiting harder. "Hey Laura. What time is it? How long til pizza?"

"Nearly time." Laura sang out from the kitchen, then she came back in and sat on the sofa. "I'm starving." She smiled across at Julia.

"OK, will you stop going on about it." He checked the time on his watch, as there was a knock on the door.

"You don't have to pay for it, it goes on my account." Julia stood up. "Do you want me to answer the door?"

"No. Sit down, and shut the fuck up. You're just like your brother, never stop talking." He pushed himself up and walked to the door. He opened it, and held his arms out to take the pizza boxes, then seemed to take off. He passed the sofa, and landed on the floor.

Pizza boxes flew after him, closely followed by Florian, who rained down punches and as many blows as he could, until the man seemed to slump. He sat back and looked at Julia and Laura.

"Hey. You both OK?" He smiled. The man opened his eyes and reared up, punching Florian squarely in his face. Blood exploded from his nose.

"Fuck. You bitch. You knew he was coming. He's a grass. Half of Moss Side got nicked after he left. Fucking grassed us all up. I was his friend, He sold me just like he sold those fuckers who jumped him." Florian grunted and started to push himself up. "No." He aimed a hard kick at her brother's stomach, and watched him roll over. "Stay down."

"He didn't grass you." The voice came from outside the open door, and blew in on the cold air. "I did. You have a problem with that? I told the police about you, because he was on the way to meet you, when he was grabbed. You knew where he'd be, nobody else. You put him in danger, and you knew he would be lucky to get out alive. Some friend you are."

"Who is that?" He looked at Julia, she recognized the voice, but she shrugged, like she had no clue.

"You going to hide in there all night?" The voice drifted in again.

"You want me, come on in." He pulled out a gun, from his waistband, and held it out in front of him. His eyes were starting to swell from the beating he had taken from Florian.

"No, please, put the gun away. My brother would never grass anyone up. He wouldn't. If you knew him at all, you know that's true." Julia shouted.

"Shut up." He turned the gun towards her, levelled at her heart. "Shut the fuck up."

"Stop. Put the gun down. Please. Let's talk about this. My brother is here. I know he didn't tell the police about you. Let's talk about it." She sat on the very edge of the sofa, and she felt, more than saw, that Laura moved away from her. She knew this man better, and believed he was capable of shooting.

"I will talk to your grass of a brother, when he wakes up." He shifted his gaze to Laura. "Shut the door. Now." She jumped up and did as she was told. "Now both of you sit down and shut up." He tucked the gun back into his waistband, and checked on Florian, who seemed to be completely unconscious. "Now, you ordered pizza, so let's eat. He picked up the pizza boxes from the floor, and opened them on the table in front of the sofa. Laura carefully picked up a slice of the vegetable one. The cheese was stringy and it looked lovely. Julia realized how hungry she was, and took a slice too. He picked up a slice of the other pizza and pulled off the pepperoni to drop into his mouth. They ate in silence, and after two slices Julia felt better, despite the circumstances. She waggled her fingers at the others and offered to fetch kitchen roll to wipe them. He nodded his permission and she stood, crossing the room. She saw a flicker of movement in the corner of her eye. Was Florian coming around, perhaps? She grabbed the kitchen roll, and searched her mind for a way to engage the others attention, rather than have them notice Florian's tiny movements.

"How long have you known my brother, Laura?" Julia smiled and hoped she looked curious, maybe even a little bit gossipy.

"Um, we were together about six months, he only told me that he had a sister just before he went away, at the start of the summer. Then when he came back, he didn't say much, he could be like that sometimes, quiet and moody, you know. Not all the time." She looked cautiously across the table at the man.

"Oh right. So how did you know to come and look for me?" She turned to face her.

"The only thing he said when he got back, was that he'd been all the way as far as you could go before you got to America. When we started looking for where he might be, we looked on Air B&B and your face was on your advert. You look so like him, it jumped out at me. We booked and came down. We still weren't sure it was you until we arrived, and then when we saw you, we knew." She smiled, showing a smile that had been whitened beyond what was natural.

"Ah. I didn't realize we were so alike, I suppose it's always harder to see it yourself." Julia shot a smile at the other woman.

"Enough! Will you two shut up!" He slammed his hand down on the table. "Laura. Help me lift him off the floor." She ran to the other side of Florian, and between them they struggled to lift him onto a hard backed chair. "Wake up." He slapped Florian's face, sending his head flopping sideways. Julia gasped.

"Please don't do that. Please. I know you're angry, but please, he's out cold, please don't hit him more." Julia begged, she stood up, and crossed the room. "Please. I'll tell you whatever I know, ask me. I might know whatever it is you're looking for without realizing it."

He turned towards her. She kept her eyes steady on his face. If ever Florian was going to make a move this was the time, but he stayed where he was. She didn't see him move, but she felt the contact of the back of his hand with her cheek. Her head snapped sideways, and her body followed. She landed in a heap.

"Stay out of my way." He meant it. She could see spit gathering at the sides of his mouth, he was furious. His arm pulled back, ready to hit Florian again. She jumped up, her head spinning and dragging at the sudden movement.

"No." She jumped and grabbed his arm, swinging her whole weight on it. He swatted her away like an annoying fly. She landed on the floor again, hearing the door swing open behind her.

"Who the fuck are you?" He shouted.

"I'm the father of the woman you just hit. I'm also the one who grassed you and your scumbag friends in Moss Side. I may also be the last thing you see." He stepped across Julia and threw himself and his fists into the argument.

They pushed and shoved, fists flying and both sporting blood on their faces. Laura slid to the ground behind the sofa. Julia tried to stand, her head feeling the size of a pumpkin, unable to think. She lifted her body as fast as she could, but it was slow. The two men were still knocking lumps out of each other. She rested her elbows on the arm of the sofa, and heaved. The man pushed her father, and he lost his footing, slipping for a second, losing concentration. Long enough for the man to pull his gun out. He pointed it at Julia, and held it.

"Everybody stay still, or Julia dies." Her Father's hand was resting on the back of a chair, Florian opened his eyes and met Julia's. He moved his eyebrow and then his eyes to his right, showing Julia which way he planned to move. She saw what he would do, judging he would put himself between her and the gun, she pleaded with everything in her eyes for him to stay still.

"Nobody's going to move. Please, calm down. Nobody is going to do anything at all. You're in charge, ask the questions you want answered. Everyone is listening, and you'll get the truth." She met his eyes, and watched the decision being made.

"I want to know who grassed me up."

"I told you, that was me. I pulled my son out of the back room of a shop, where he had been beaten, burned, tortured. Those people deserved to serve some time. You were the one he went to meet that day, supposed to be his friend. Nobody knew where he would be except you. You put him in that room, you deserved it too." He stepped towards the gun. "So, if you want to shoot someone, shoot me."

"Stand still." His voice wavered a little.

"No. My daughter is nothing to do with this. This is me, and you." He rubbed his hand over his lip, wiping away the blood. "Why don't we let the girls go, and settle this between us. We don't need them getting in the way."

"Laura is here because she used to be in love with your son. Not anymore. She wanted to know why he ran out on her, and never phoned or emailed. I am here, to kill him, and probably you too, but I know that there is something in this room which is more precious to you than your life. So, I am going to kill Julia first, and you are going to watch. Later, I will kill you." His nose was dripping blood, and he was laughing,

Julia watched him, then she took a step towards him. She didn't know why. His eyes changed. There was a moment, maybe less than that, when his attention was taken, and that was enough. Florian left the chair, and barged the man to the side, Julia watched the gun, which pointed at her then up at the ceiling, and then she watched the arc it made back towards her. There was a sound behind her, but she was too focused on watching the gun to hear it properly. Then there was a noise, an explosion which seemed to fill the room. She waited for pain, but there was none. Then the man crumpled, like he had been folded in the middle. The gun dropped, the man dropped, there was noise, then someone was holding her. She turned her head, to look behind her, and saw her mother, with a gun in her hand.

"What happened?" Her voice was a whisper.

"We have to move. Florian, come on. Katya, good shot my love." He leaned down to kiss her. He reached over to pull his son up, there was blood everywhere, it was all over Florian.

"Florian? Are you hurt?" Julia reached out to him.

231

"No, I'm fine. Come on. Let's get out of here. Laura. Come on." He reached his hand out and pulled Laura out from behind the sofa.

They walked out together, into the cool early evening. Julia felt her father's arm around her, and her mother's hand resting on her arm. She saw her brother wrap his arms around Laura, and took what felt like her first breath in hours.

"What happened to Gemma? I got a call through to her, why didn't she turn up? I thought the police would be coming in through the windows." Julia stepped through her own front door and found herself in the middle of puppy frenzy.

"Gemma was trying to get firearms support. I knew he would be armed. She couldn't get permission to go in until she had armed back up. So, we came in to get you out. She sort of agreed to it, at least, I don't think she'll be prosecuting, especially as we only talked our way in, and managed to get hold of one of his guns." Florian fixed her with a hard look, and nodded to her slowly. She found that she was nodding too.

"Yeah, what happened with Gemma?" Laura asked.

"Gemma is a local police officer. Not Florian's new girlfriend." Julia explained. The front door opened, and Ben walked in with Gemma. "Ben!" She ran across the room and threw herself into his arms.

"No more of this. I can't take any more. If we have to sell up and go and live somewhere else, we do it. I don't want you in danger again, Julia." He looked over her shoulder, at Florian.

"I need to know what happened in there, but first, is anyone hurt?" Gemma was all business.

"I think we all need a little something for the shock." Alex passed small glasses of brandy around to every one of them. "Gemma, I am sorry. Part of my deal with the police was giving details of a drug gang in Manchester, and it appears that people have assumed that it was Florian who gave them up, because he disappeared at the same time. It's my fault, Julia. I put you in danger, and could have lost you. Tell me what to do, Gemma, to keep them all safe."

Laura sunk into a chair. "When Florian disappeared, he kept coming to my flat, asking me where he had gone, and what he was up to. Then people started being arrested, and Dave, you know, who looked after your dad when he stayed in Manchester, he died, people were saying that Florian killed him, but it was an overdose, I went to the hospital and they told me. There were rumours flying all over the place. It was mad, then Billy turned up at my place, and he said he wanted to talk to me, that he was worried about you. I was scared, you saw how he was. I told him everything I knew, then he started looking at places to stay down here, and your face popped up, Julia on the advert. You look so like Florian, it was simple. I haven't talked to anyone else about it, and he was with me from when I talked to him, til now. Nobody else knows you're here. Just take down your photo, for god's sake." She sipped her brandy, and nodded.

"I've missed you, L." Florian pulled her close.

"Then have a bath, you're covered in Billy." She laughed, and pushed him away. Her hands less shaky and her voice stronger.

"Right. Nobody is to go into the holiday let, I have forensic people coming. I need statements from every one of you, and Ben, you need to put the kettle on, or they will all be drunk and they will make no sense." Gemma sent Ben off to the kitchen. She waited until her was out of the room, and lowered her voice. "Who shot the lovely Billy then?"

"It was me. He was going to shoot my daughter, and there was a gun on the little table, so I picked it up and shot him." She met the glare that Gemma had been perfecting since the day she started at police training.

233

"Is that what everybody saw?" Gemma looked at the others, who nodded except for Laura.

"I didn't see anything. I was hiding behind the couch." Laura met the glare too.

"Right, make those statements, take your time, and I am going to speak to my boss, and probably his boss, and maybe bosses beyond that, because I don't know what is supposed to happen next. Either way, she's right, you need to get cleaned up, and have a good night's rest if you can. Laura, are you happy to stay here, or would you like me to arrange accommodation for you?" Gemma raised an eyebrow at her.

"I'd like to stay." She looked at Florian.

"She can stay at mine tonight." He confirmed.

"OK, I am not going to take statements now, I think this has been traumatic enough for one day. I will come up here tomorrow at nine and we'll start then." She showed herself out, shouting her goodbyes to Ben.

"Alexei. It's OK, all the family is here now. Everybody is safe. We're going to be fine." She patted her husband on the shoulder, and smiled when he raised his head. "Florian, go and have a shower. I will make some food, and then we will sit down to eat like proper people. I was proud of you all today." She bustled off to the kitchen, chatting happily to the puppy and pulling food out of the cupboards and the fridge.

Ben brought in the coffees and passed them round, but nobody drank much of them. He stayed close to Julia, and watched her face, while her Father and Laura chatted about Florian and he told her stories about the rest of the family. Ben draped his arm over Julia's shoulders, and he breathed a sigh of relief.

Julia turned when she felt him sigh. He was watching her, and his eyes shone. Her smile widened, and she closed the distance between them to meet his lips with hers. She was lucky, in so many ways, and whatever the future brought, she knew that, having tied up all the loose ends with her family and everything else, she was ready to deal with whatever came next.

Printed in Great Britain
by Amazon

38973261R00133